"Great, Will," Jessica said in a flat tone. "You know, I *was* ready to be friends with you, but I can't take this. I need you to give me some space here. You're gonna have to stop playing stalker."

Will tucked his chin and sighed. The crowd in the hall was thinning out, and she glanced at her watch. "Okay," he said. "I'll leave you alone. But I'm not the jerk you think I am."

"Whatever. I have to go." And with that, Jessica turned and walked into her class without even saying good-bye.

"I'm not giving up," Will said quietly.

He turned to head for his next class and froze. Melissa was standing just down the hall, her blue eyes wide, clutching her notebook to her chest as if she was trying to hold herself together.

Oh God, Will thought. *How much did she hear?*

"Melissa—," Will said.

But before he could even think of anything to say, she turned on her heel and ran out the back door of the school. Will closed his eyes, shaking his head slowly as the shrill late bell rang out, piercing his eardrums.

Great job, Simmons, he told himself. He'd made the two people he cared about the most miserable before he even got to second period. A perfect record.

Don't miss any of the books in SWEET VALLEY HIGH
SENIOR YEAR, an exciting new series from Bantam Books!

#1 CAN'T STAY AWAY

#2 SAY IT TO MY FACE

#3 SO COOL

#4 I'VE GOT A SECRET

#5 IF YOU ONLY KNEW

#6 YOUR BASIC NIGHTMARE

#7 BOY MEETS GIRL

#8 MARIA WHO?

#9 THE ONE THAT GOT AWAY

Visit the Official Sweet Valley Web Site on the Internet at:

http://www.sweetvalley.com

Francine Pascal's SVH senior year

The One That Got Away

CREATED BY
FRANCINE PASCAL

BANTAM BOOKS
NEW YORK · TORONTO · LONDON · SYDNEY · AUCKLAND

RL 6, age 12 and up

THE ONE THAT GOT AWAY

A Bantam Book / October 1999

Sweet Valley High® *is a registered trademark of Francine Pascal.*
Conceived by Francine Pascal.
Cover photography by Michael Segal.

Produced by 17th Street Productions,
a division of Daniel Weiss Associates, Inc.
33 West 17th Street
New York, NY 10011.

ISBN: 0-553-49281-0

Published simultaneously in the United States and Canada

PRINTED IN THE UNITED STATES OF AMERICA

OPM   0 9 8 7 6 5 4 3 2 1

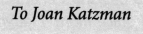

To Joan Katzman

Jeremy Aames

For the first time, I have a real girlfriend.

I mean, I've dated girls before, but Jessica is everything a girlfriend is supposed to be. She's changed my entire life. I smile more. I laugh more. And not only when she's around. Just in general. Like knowing she's out there, being my girlfriend, makes everything easier.

I don't know how I would have gotten through all this stuff without her. And right now, I don't know how I would get through a regular day without her.

I hope I never have to find out.

Will Simmons

I feel like my life is mine again. I never realized how much I was tiptoeing around Melissa, censoring everything I did so I wouldn't upset her, down to what kind of pizza to order. I don't even remember what kind of pizza I like. It's been so long since anybody asked.

Most people would think I'm insane for wanting to start up another relationship right away. I probably am insane, but with Jessica, I can't help myself. Jessica is not Melissa.

Jessica is very, very different.

Jessica Wakefield

Getting crushed, dissed, and generally humiliated by Will Simmons taught me a lesson. It made me appreciate a really nice guy like Jeremy Aames.

Okay. The fact that Jeremy is drop-dead gorgeous doesn't exactly hurt. But that's not why I'm with him. Really. It's because he's a wonderful person who really cares about me. The resemblance to Tom Cruise is purely coincidental.

When I was so sure I was in love with Will Simmons, I didn't know a thing about him except that he was cool, cocky, and good-looking. And look where it got me.

Well, I'm done with acting on impulse. My relationship with Jeremy is perfect. And I'm not doing anything to screw it up.

Ever.

CHAPTER 1
Thanks, but No Thanks

"Surprise," Will Simmons said softly. He tried to smile, but he was too nervous. A light mist was turning into a heavy drizzle. The coliseum lights shone on Jessica Wakefield's rain-slicked features, highlighting her perfect cheekbones, blue-green eyes, and glossy blond hair, and he took a step closer. Only then did he notice the look on her face.

He had been prepared for her to be angry at him. He had hoped she'd be excited. But he hadn't expected disgusted horror. He also hadn't counted on an audience. Jessica's twin sister, Elizabeth, and their friend Tia Ramirez were standing right behind Jessica. They glanced at each other, their eyes wide with wary surprise.

Well, there's no turning back now, Will thought. He took a deep breath and pulled a bunch of red roses from behind his back.

Jessica took a step back, as if he were holding out a knife. "You're kidding me, right?"

"No," Will said. "These are for you."

"I don't want them," Jessica answered evenly. "I

1

don't want anything from you." Her narrow-eyed look of anger left him speechless.

"*You're* the one who's been leaving me all those presents?" she demanded. "Is this your idea of some sick joke? Haven't you done enough to me already?" Jessica glared at him, ignoring the rain dripping down her face like angry tears.

"No! It's not like that. I just wanted to . . . talk to you." He glanced at Tia and Elizabeth, and they looked away.

"I should have known it was you!" she said bitterly. "It's like messing with my head is one of your favorite pastimes."

"Jess—"

"I can't believe you," she continued. "You said you just wanted to be friends! And the whole time you were leaving me notes, setting me up to meet you here . . . and then what? Have a good laugh with your friends because I fell for it?" She tossed her head, causing a spray of droplets to flash in the harsh fluorescent lights.

Will gave her a second to make sure she was done. She just stood there and glared at him.

"Okay," Will said. "Can I just say something?" He stood stiffly, the roses hanging at his side.

"No. You can't," Jessica said. "Just stay away from me. I've had it with you and your psycho girlfriend."

"She's not my girlfriend," Will said numbly.

"Right. For how long?" Jessica said sarcastically.

"Wait. You know what? It doesn't matter. Because I don't care."

"You don't understand," Will said, clenching his teeth. "I broke up with her because of you."

"So, now you're blaming me?" Jessica held up her hand. "I'm not getting in the middle again."

He swallowed hard and looked down at his soggy sneakers. "What I'm trying to say is . . ." He paused. He hated doing this in front of all of them, but if he didn't say it now, he might never get another chance. "Ever since I met you, I knew I had to be with you." He looked up and saw three mouths gaping at him. "Give me another chance?"

"Are you out of your mind?" Jessica looked like she was ready to spit flames. "After what you two did to me, you expect me to go *out* with you? Do you really think a few presents and some cheesy poetry are going to make me forget the whole school was calling me a slut?"

"I told you I'm sorry about all that," Will said, trying to stay calm.

"And you know I have a boyfriend!" Jessica continued as if he hadn't spoken. "What did you think I was going to do—sneak around behind his back? Just because you cheat on your girlfriend doesn't mean I'm the same way!"

"What are you doing here, then?" Will demanded, unable to keep the bitterness out of his voice. "Where's your boyfriend now?"

Jessica's eyes clouded.

"I came here," she said in a low voice, "to tell my secret admirer thanks but no thanks. I thought I owed him that much. If I had known it was you, I would never have come." She spun around and headed for her Jeep, which was parked by the curb with its hazards on.

Will watched, stunned, as Jessica yanked open the car door and climbed in, slamming it behind her. Tia and Elizabeth scrambled in the passenger side, and they tore off, spattering Will with muddy water. All Will could do was stare after them, too stunned to move.

Jeremy plopped the bag of groceries on the kitchen counter and sank into a chair, rubbing his temples. At least he'd made it home. His car had been running on empty, but he hadn't had enough money for gas after picking up the groceries. If his mom couldn't come up with a few bucks, he wasn't sure his car would make it to school tomorrow.

Oh, well, tomorrow was tomorrow. All he could do was take one day at a time. At least now there was hope.

He forced himself to get up, put away the groceries, and start boiling some water on the stove.

"Jeremy!" His six-year-old sister, Trisha, ran up to him. He bent down, and she gave him a sloppy kiss.

"How you doin', squirt?" he said.

4

She beamed at him. "Look what I drew!" she said proudly, thrusting a messy drawing at him.

"Wow! Hey, I'm putting that right on the refrigerator," he said, giving her a hug. He opened a kitchen drawer and tore two tiny pieces of tape off a slim roll.

"Are you hungry?" Jeremy asked. "I'm making your favorite, macaroni and cheese."

"Surprise, surprise." Jeremy looked up to see his twelve-year-old sister, Emma, standing in the doorway with her arms crossed. "What does that make, the third time this week? Are we going for a world record or something?"

"Hey, we've got a case of the stuff. We might as well use it, right?" Jeremy answered.

"Why can't we eat something good?" Emma demanded. "I'm sick of eating the same thing all the time. Oatmeal for breakfast. Peanut butter for lunch. Mac-'n'-cheese for dinner. I can't remember the last time we had steak."

"Funny you should say that," Jeremy said, breaking out into a grin. He opened the refrigerator and whipped out a large, shrink-wrapped package. "You just guessed course number two!" With his other hand he held out a bottle of sparkling cider. "Anyone care for a little champagne first?"

"What's going on?" Emma asked suspiciously.

"We're celebrating," Jeremy said. He popped the top off the cider bottle and filled three glasses.

"Here's to Dad's new job!" He clicked the plastic rim of his glass against the top of his sisters' cups, and they both giggled.

"Are we having cake for dessert too?" Trisha asked, clapping.

"No. But how about if we bake some cookies?" Jeremy said.

"Yippee! Chocolate-chip cookies!" shouted Trisha.

Jeremy opened the cupboard and examined the barren shelves. Except for the bread and peanut butter he had just bought, there wasn't much there. Splurging on steak had cleaned him out. "Hmmm. We seem to be out of chocolate chips right now," he said.

"We're out of everything," Emma grumbled.

"I know," Jeremy said. "How about peanut-butter cookies?"

"Yay!" Trisha cheered.

"Cool. We can surprise Mom when she gets home." Jeremy handed Emma the cookbook, and to his relief, after a brief hesitation she opened it.

Jeremy felt his shoulders untense. Now, assuming they had enough flour, sugar, butter, and eggs, he would be able to keep his sisters happy and occupied until his mother got home. Then maybe he could finally do a little homework before crashing.

He rubbed his hands over his face and sighed. It was getting harder and harder to keep the whole happy-family thing going. But if his dad's new job panned out, things would start getting back to normal. He knocked on the wooden cutting board for luck.

On impulse Jeremy reached for the phone and dialed Jessica's number. It had been so long since he'd had anything happy to tell her, he couldn't wait to share the good news about the venture-capital firm that had decided to invest in his dad's company.

"Fowler residence. How may I help you?" a cold, formal voice answered.

"Uh, yes, this is Jeremy Aames. Is Jessica Wakefield there, please?" It always made him uncomfortable to speak to the Fowlers' servants.

"Jessica is not in. May I take a message?"

"No, thanks." Jeremy hung up the phone, disappointed. He could have sworn Jessica had said she was going to stay home and study tonight.

Oh, well, Jeremy thought, trying to keep up his energy. *It'll still be good news later.*

"Are you okay, Jess?" Elizabeth asked, glancing at her sister from the front passenger seat.

"I'm fine," Jessica said. A drop of water dripped from her wet hair into her right eye, and she wiped it away. The rain was still coming down hard outside, and she was driving fast. She turned abruptly, sending a spray of water onto the sidewalk.

"Maybe you should slow down a little," Elizabeth said. Jessica ignored her.

"I can't believe your secret admirer turned out to be Will," Tia said, leaning over from the backseat so she could be heard. "I'm still in shock."

"I know. He's insane," Jessica said. "He spreads lies about me all over school, then he expects me to go out with him. How egotistical can you get?" She bit her lip, remembering the look on his face when he had arrived at the theater. He had looked anything but conceited tonight. Hopeful, eager—maybe even a bit nervous. Not at all like that first week of school, when he had been so obviously sure that he was going to be running the place. Jessica flushed as she remembered Will standing over her in the Fowlers' family room, his eyes burning into her as he leaned forward and they kissed—

"Look out!" Elizabeth shouted.

Jessica looked up just in time to swerve out of the way of a delivery truck backing out of a driveway. "Jess? Are you sure you're okay?" Elizabeth asked. "Maybe I should drive."

"I'm fine," Jessica replied, gasping for breath. Her heart was pounding like a jackhammer, and it wasn't just because of their near collision.

"Seeing Will really rattled you, huh?" Elizabeth said.

"Of course it did!" Jessica snapped, gripping the wheel tightly and peering out into the rainy night. "Why can't he just leave me alone?"

"I'm surprised he had the guts to show his face

after what he and Melissa put you through," Tia said, leaning against the back of Jessica's seat.

Elizabeth turned to face them. "I don't know. That was more Melissa than Will. Besides, he apologized for that already, didn't he?"

"What?" Tia asked, almost hitting her head on the roof. "When did this happen? How could you not tell me?"

"He came by the house the other day," Jessica admitted, keeping an eye on the road. "He asked if I thought I could ever be friends with him."

"And you didn't think this was worth mentioning?" Tia said. "Come on, give it up. What did you tell him?"

Jessica sighed in frustration. "I said it was possible. *Possible!* How was I supposed to know he would pull a stupid stunt like this?"

Elizabeth raised an eyebrow and stared at her curiously. "Are you sure you're not being a little hard on the guy? Maybe he really does like you. I mean, what if he meant all that stuff he said?"

Jessica stomped on the gas pedal, and Elizabeth winced. "Please! Will hasn't been honest with me once since the day I met him," Jessica fumed, passing a minivan on the right. "First he dates me behind Melissa's back—conveniently forgetting to tell me that he already has a girlfriend. Then when she finds out, he denies the whole thing and claims I came on to him. Then he stands by while she turns all my friends against me and spreads rumors all over school. Now, when his girlfriend completely loses it, he decides he wants to be with me. And I'm supposed to be flattered?" She snorted. "He's not even straightforward about that! No, he has to leave a bunch of secret notes and gifts, then ambush me. And remember, this is right after he says he just wants to be friends. I'm sorry—I don't care if he sends me a truckload of diamonds. I don't need him. I found somebody ten times better than him anyway."

A dull ache that felt suspiciously like longing started to emanate from Jessica's heart. She forced herself to focus on the anger.

"Don't get me wrong—Jeremy is great," Elizabeth agreed, shifting in her seat. She hesitated, then continued. "I was just saying, Will seemed like he felt pretty bad about what happened. I think he really cares about you."

Tia rolled her eyes. "Yeah, right," she said.

"Will doesn't care about anybody but himself," Jessica agreed, spraying water on a motorcycle as she sped past. "Jeremy is worth ten of him."

"Yeah, come on, Liz," Tia said, turning toward her. "His girlfriend just got out of the hospital, and he starts hitting on the person she hates the most? I'm sorry. The guy's got no class." She tossed her dark hair in disgust.

"Exactly," Jessica said. But her heart was still

pounding with the memory of his kiss, and she felt like a liar. "All Will does is make me appreciate how lucky I am to have a great boyfriend like Jeremy." She licked her lips, as if to wipe away the memory of Will's kiss.

"You know what?" she said impulsively. "I'm going to drop you guys off and go visit Jeremy right now."

"Sounds like a plan," Tia said quickly.

Jessica rolled her shoulders back in an attempt to loosen the knots that had rapidly formed there. *Forget about Will,* she told herself. It was time to start concentrating on someone worth caring about. And there was no one more worthy of her time than Jeremy.

Melissa Fox

Essay:
Name a book that has had an important
effect on you, and explain why.

When I was a little girl, my mother gave me a book of Aesop's Fables. I studied the pictures as if they contained all the secrets to my future. The story I liked best was about the tortoise and the hare because the moral was "slow and steady wins the race."

I was smaller than the other girls back then, and I was plain looking and awkward. I wasn't bubbly and fun loving like the popular girls, and no one noticed me. But that story convinced me I would get what I wanted in the end.

When I was in second grade, my dad took me to a football game, and I made up my mind that I was going to be a cheerleader. My parents thought this was cute, and they gave me a tiny cheerleading outfit. They would laugh at me standing in front of the mirror and practicing for hours every day. But I was dead serious about it.

I studied the older girls and copied all of their moves. I didn't tell any of my friends about my plan except Cherie. I convinced her we were both going to be cheerleaders someday, and I taught her everything I'd learned until she was almost as good as me.

When the junior-high

cheerleading tryouts finally arrived, a lot of people were surprised I went out for the team. But when my turn came, I could tell everyone was impressed.

I pretended not to care. I just went back and helped Cherie with her routine. I knew the other girls were watching, but I ignored them. Finally, just as I had predicted, one of them asked me to show her what I was teaching Cherie. Before long they were all coming to me for advice. I helped them all, except the most popular one. Soon I was the new leader of the group.

A lot of people think the race goes to the swift and the battle to the strong. They're wrong. I have one piece of advice for the front-runners in life: watch your back.

CHAPTER
Slave Drivers
2

Angel Desmond hoisted a tray of empty glasses and held it over his head, trying to maneuver through the crowded second floor of the Riot. Cold, sticky liquid from a spilled drink dribbled from the tray down his arm, but there was nothing he could do about it. It didn't matter anyway. His black T-shirt and jeans were already covered with damp stains. He swung open the door to the kitchen and deposited the tray on the rack by the dishwasher, then paused and wiped his hands on his thighs.

"What's the matter? Nothing to do?" Angel jumped at the sound of his boss's voice behind him. "This isn't break time. What are you standing around for? Get out to the bar and help Jason."

Angel clenched his teeth and hurried through the swinging doors to the bar. Jason grunted an exhausted greeting, and Angel wordlessly started serving drinks as fast as he could. When the crowd finally thinned a bit, he wiped the sweat off his forehead and saw Conner coming up the stairs. Angel lifted his chin in acknowledgment, then glanced nervously over his shoulder and returned to work.

Conner sauntered over and slid wearily onto a stool at the far end of the bar, where Jason took his order for a Coke. Angel looked around, then walked over. He grabbed a dishrag and started wiping the bar in front of Conner. "Sorry I can't talk," he muttered. "The boss is watching me like a hawk."

Conner shrugged and took a sip of his drink.

"He's always spying on us," Angel continued as he wiped the back of his hand across his forehead again. "You can work nonstop for an hour, and as soon as you pause for one second, he throws a fit."

"So quit," Conner said.

"I can't." Angel frowned and scrubbed harder. "My dad cut my hours at the garage, and I need all the work I can get here to save money for school." A rivulet of sweat meandered down the smooth, dark skin of his neck. "If I want to come down from Stanford to visit Tia on the weekends, I'm going to have to save a lot of money." A shadow passed over his brown eyes. "Of course, I hardly have any time to see her *now*."

A customer set an empty glass on the bar, and Angel grabbed it and put it on a tray. "What are you doing up here alone?" Angel asked.

Conner sighed. "I couldn't take all the yakking. Remind me never to go out with a bunch of girls again."

"Is Tia down there?" Angel asked.

"Yeah. And a couple of cheerleaders," Conner said. "That was bad enough, but then Tia said Maria was meeting her here, so I split."

Angel wondered if it was really Maria that Conner was worried about seeing or if he was concerned Maria might bring Elizabeth.

"You seem kind of down, man. Is something wrong?" Angel asked.

Conner scowled. "Yeah. I'm sick of everybody asking me what's wrong. In the entire time you've known me, have I ever said I had a problem I wanted to talk about?"

Angel grabbed a peanut from a bowl on the bar, tossed it in the air, and caught it in his mouth. "Not that I can think of," he said with a grin.

Conner scratched his unshaven cheek, then ran his hands through his scruffy dark hair. "Look, I didn't mean to go off on you," he said. "I guess I just feel like being alone."

"Angel!" came a shout from across the room. "Quit talking to the customers!"

"Got your wish," Angel replied. He started working his way down the bar, cleaning up half-empty glasses and soaked cardboard coasters.

Conner stood up, threw down a tip, and walked along the other side of the bar. "This place is too noisy anyway. I'm going to a movie."

"What are you gonna see?" Angel asked without looking up.

"Who cares? Whatever's dark and empty. Catch you later." He reached over and slapped Angel's hand.

"Angel!" Jason called. "The boss needs you. Someone spilled a tray of coffee. He said to bring a mop."

"Coming," Angel said, watching Conner slouch toward the door. Conner was obviously upset about something, but Angel couldn't help envying him. Whatever was eating the guy couldn't be as bad as spending the next three hours as slave labor.

Jessica felt her chest tightening as she approached Jeremy's door. She'd already decided that telling him about her encounter with Will would only upset him. He had enough on his mind. But making that decision didn't lessen the guilt she felt over hiding something from him. She did her best to calm her nerves and rang the doorbell.

Seconds later Jeremy opened the door and a warm, comforting smell wafted out. "I can't believe it!" he said with a huge smile. Unfortunately the sight of his handsome face made her feel even worse. "I just called you. You must have been on your way over."

"I had a sudden urge to see you," Jessica said as casually as possible. She stood on her toes and gave him a quick kiss.

"Come on in," he said, ushering her through the door as she slipped out of her raincoat. Jeremy took the jacket from her and shook about a gallon of water onto the tiled foyer floor. "What have you been doing? Jogging around in the rain?"

Jessica's stomach turned, but she managed a tight laugh in response to his joke as he hung up her coat. "So, what were you calling me about?" she asked as he wrapped his arms around her waist.

Jeremy smiled, looking happier than she'd seen him in days. "I have some good news," he said. "You know that friend of my dad's who's starting a new company and wants my dad to work with him?"

"Right. You told me about that the other day," Jessica said.

"Well, they did it," Jeremy said, his eyes gleaming. "They nailed a big investor."

"That's great!" Jessica cried, throwing her arms around his neck and giving him a huge hug. He hugged her back tightly, and it seemed to squeeze some of the heavy feeling out of her. "When does he start working?"

"He's meeting with them right now. They're still working on getting the rest of the financing together, but it looks really good." He smiled and pushed her wet hair behind her ears. "Isn't it funny how everything started to go better once I met you? I think I'll start calling you my guardian angel," he said, leaning over to kiss her lightly on the neck.

Jessica's heart thumped painfully. "Please. I'm no angel," she said, fighting the urge to push him away. *What would he think if he knew where I was just now?*

That's crazy, she reminded herself. She had done nothing wrong. There was no way she could have known her secret admirer was going to be Will. Besides, she had done exactly what she went there to do. She'd told her secret admirer she had a boyfriend and wasn't interested. The whole thing was over and done with.

Then why do I still feel guilty? she thought.

"Is something wrong?" Jeremy said. "You seem a little tense."

She sighed. He hadn't known her very long, and he could already read her. Jessica shrugged, avoiding his gaze. "I'm just a little tired, I guess."

Jeremy pulled away and then casually threw his arm over her shoulders. "I have the perfect remedy for that," he said, leading her toward the kitchen. "Lots and lots of sugar."

He pushed open the kitchen door. Sitting in the middle of the floor with a cookie in each hand was a chubby six-year-old girl.

"This is Trisha," Jeremy said. "Trish, this is my friend Jessica."

"Want a cookie?" Trisha said, offering Jessica one of hers.

"Thanks!" Jessica said, smiling as she knelt down to take the cookie. She looked up at Jeremy. "She could be your twin."

"Right. Just female and about eleven years behind," Jeremy said.

Just then an older girl with braces and long, brown braids burst into the room. She huffed over to the kitchen counter, plopped down on a stool, and dropped a pile of books on the counter with a bang. "Who's she?" the girl asked, finally looking up.

Jeremy leveled her with a glare. "Emma, this is my friend Jessica."

Emma's gaze quickly flicked over Jessica from head to toe. "Are you Jeremy's girlfriend?"

"Emma—," Jeremy began.

"I don't know," Jessica said, looking Jeremy over. "I'm still deciding."

Emma smiled. "Get out while you can. You should see what he looks like when he gets up in the morning."

Jessica felt her cheeks turn bright red and saw Jeremy's do the same. "I like her," Jessica said.

"That makes one of us," Jeremy quipped. He strolled across the room and looked over Emma's shoulder at her open notebook. "How's your math homework going, Em?"

"Okay." She tore a corner off her paper, then another. "I just don't feel like doing it right now."

"Come on, let's get it over with," Jeremy said, pulling up a stool. "Then you can go watch TV."

"I can't do it," she said, pushing away her notebook. "It's too hard."

Jeremy glanced at Jessica. "Maybe for some people it is, but not for you," he said. "It's fractions, right? Fractions are an Aames-family specialty. Here, I'll show you." They huddled over her notebook. "You don't mind, do you, Jessica?" he asked.

"No. Go ahead," Jessica said, amazed.

What was with this guy? If she had asked her brother, Steven, for help when she was little and he had had a girl over? Forget about it. She would have been lucky to escape with her life.

Trisha walked over to Jessica and grabbed her hand. "Let's draw!" she said, holding up a handful of white paper.

"Sure," Jessica said with a grin.

She hoisted Trisha onto one of the high stools and settled in next to her. As Trisha grabbed a pencil and started to scribble, Jessica snuck a look at Jeremy. He was already smiling at her. For a moment she just looked into his warm brown eyes, and that was all she needed. She knew this was where she wanted to be.

Maria Slater was closing her locker when she saw Elizabeth shuffling toward her. Elizabeth's blue cardigan sweater was misbuttoned, and she looked like she could barely drag herself down the hall.

"Liz!" Maria called. "Over here!"

Elizabeth trudged over. "If you're mad about my article, I'm really sorry," she said. "I know it was supposed to be eight hundred words, but five hundred was all I could manage. I haven't been sleeping well."

"Hey, you're still the editor in chief. You can write whatever you want," Maria said. "I just wanted to fix your sweater." Elizabeth glanced down indifferently as Maria adjusted her buttons. "It's a good thing you're wearing a T-shirt under this," she said, shaking her tight black curls back from her face.

"I'm lucky I remembered to wear a shirt at all," Elizabeth said. "I must have fallen asleep about one minute before the alarm went off. By the way, thanks for checking the layout for me again."

"Don't worry about the *Oracle,*" Maria said with a smile. "Everything's under control."

"Thanks," Elizabeth said, her eyes downcast.

Maria felt a pang of sympathy for her friend

and gave her a quick hug. She knew *exactly* what Elizabeth was feeling. Maria had had more than a few sleepless nights herself over Conner McDermott, and she was still trying to completely expunge his memory. But at least she didn't have to worry about stumbling upon Elizabeth and Conner making out in the hall anymore. He had dumped Elizabeth even more cruelly than he had Maria.

The first bell rang, and Maria pulled away. "I'll see you in class later, okay?" she said.

Elizabeth nodded wearily. "If I make it that long."

Maria cast her one last sympathetic glance and hurried off down the hall. She was about to go into her history class when she heard a male voice yell her name.

For a split second her heart leaped as she imagined it was Conner. She grimaced. When was she going to stop doing that? She looked up and saw with relief that it was Ken Matthews rushing toward her.

"Did you get my e-mail?" she asked.

"Yeah." He looked away, embarrassed. "That's what I have to talk to you about." He scratched his neck and stared at the ceiling. "I was thinking, maybe you should just do this one without me."

"What? Why?"

He kicked the floor. "You really saved me on

that last project, but I don't want to keep dragging you down."

"What are you talking about?" Maria said. "We got a B-plus."

"Yeah. But you know you would've gotten an A if I hadn't been involved," Ken said, shaking his shaggy blond hair.

Maria rolled her eyes. "Ken—"

"You don't understand. Look." He unzipped his backpack and took out his notebook. "I started to review my notes for our meeting, you know, to get ready?" He flipped through his notebook, showing her the pages. Except for a few doodles, they were all blank. "See? I guess I cut more classes than I realized, and when I did come, I wasn't really paying much attention." For the first time he looked up at her, and she could see the shame he was trying to conceal. "I mean, what's the point of even meeting with me tonight? I'd be totally useless."

"Ken." Maria took his arm and looked directly into his stormy, sea blue eyes. "If all you're worried about is not having any notes, why don't you just borrow mine?" He didn't answer. "You've got all day to go over them." She opened her backpack and pulled out her history notebook. "I'll give it to you after class."

"Okay. I'll read it, but it won't do any good," Ken said with a shrug.

"Look, you've gotta know by now that I'm not going to let you back out on me," Maria said. "So you might as well just suck it up and get to work."

Ken smirked. "All right, slave driver," he said. "But don't blame me when Harvard doesn't show up at your house with balloons and a welcome letter." He reached over and held the classroom door open for her.

"No biggie." Maria grinned as she breezed by him. "I'm all about Princeton anyway."

Jeremy Aames

I could definitely feel something weird going on with Jessica last night. I just wish I knew what it was. There was something going on behind her eyes, and when I kissed her, it was like she was forcing herself.

Maybe she was irritated about spending time with my sisters. It wasn't exactly the most romantic situation. I mean, sitting around the kitchen table doing homework? We've been together for five minutes, and we're acting like an old married couple.

Man, I really hope my dad's job works out. We could hire a baby-sitter, and I could actually use the money I make on myself . . . and on Jessica.

CHAPTER 3

Too Late

"Jessica!" Will saw her slim figure round the corner and hurried after her. He had to catch her before she got to class. "Wait!" he called.

She froze for a second, then lowered her head and kept walking. Will ran up and cut her off just before she reached the classroom door.

"Please. I just wanted to say I'm sorry," he said, trying to catch his breath.

Jessica glared at him. "For what?" she said, crossing her arms.

"I shouldn't have surprised you like that last night," he said. He ran his fingers through his hair, then stuck his hands in his pockets. "But I had no choice. I didn't think you would have come otherwise."

"You were right," Jessica said.

Will inhaled sharply and shifted his weight to his other foot. "I was just trying to do something nice."

Jessica took a deep breath too. "How am I supposed to believe that after everything that's happened?"

31

"Look, I know I screwed up—"

She fixed him with a skeptical glare.

"Big time," he finished. "But I'm sorry. I just wish you would trust me."

She looked at the ground, causing her fine blond hair to fall forward and cover her cheeks. It was all Will could do to keep himself from reaching up and gently tucking the golden strands behind her ear. Finally she looked up again, breaking him out of his trance.

"If you want me to trust you, then you're going to have to stop putting so much pressure on me," she said, her stunning, blue-green eyes wary and clouded. "I mean, I have a *boyfriend*. How did you *think* I was going to react? Did you even think about anyone but yourself?"

Will could smell the faint, flowery scent of her shampoo, and for a second he couldn't speak. "I guess I was just hoping . . . ," he said hoarsely. He'd been hoping she would be overjoyed to see him. He'd been hoping she would just fall into his arms. But he couldn't exactly say that now. "I don't know," he finished lamely.

"Great, Will," Jessica said in a flat tone. "You know, I *was* ready to be friends with you, but I can't take this. I need you to give me some space here. You're gonna have to stop playing stalker."

Will tucked his chin and sighed. The crowd in the hall was thinning out, and she glanced at her watch. "Okay," he said. "I'll leave you alone. But I'm not the jerk you think I am."

"Whatever. I have to go." And with that, Jessica turned and walked into her class without even saying good-bye.

Will just stood there for a moment, staring at the closed door. How had things gone so completely wrong?

"I'm not giving up," he said quietly.

He turned to head for his next class and froze. Melissa was standing just down the hall, her blue eyes wide, clutching her notebook to her chest as if she was trying to hold herself together.

Oh God, Will thought. *How much did she hear?*

"Melissa—," Will said.

But before he could even think of anything to say, she turned on her heel and ran out the back door of the school.

Will closed his eyes, shaking his head slowly as the shrill late bell rang out, piercing his eardrums.

Great job, Simmons, he told himself. He'd made the two people he cared about the most miserable before he even got to second period. A perfect record.

When the bell rang to end class, Jessica was startled. Had an hour really passed already? She looked at her notebook. The page was blank. She hadn't stopped thinking about Will for the whole hour. So much for putting him out of her mind.

Jessica got up in a daze and wandered into the hallway, trying to recall what the lecture had been about. Something about doomed lovers, but which ones? Romeo and Juliet? Desdemona and Othello? Helena and Demetrius? She didn't even know which play they were reading. *Great, Jess,* she thought. *Way to focus on the important.*

Suddenly a low whistle sliced through her thoughts.

"Hey, where's your miniskirt, Wakefield?"

Jessica felt her face flush instantly and wished for the thousandth time that she had control over her blood vessels. It was bad enough that they continued to pick on her. She hated the fact that the effect they had was obvious.

She lifted her head and looked at her attacker. A big, blond jock was leering at her from across the hall. "Forgot which car you left it in last night?" He cackled, looking just like one of those idiot guests on a daytime talk show.

Jessica turned her back on him and walked away. The catcalls were coming much less frequently now, but they still hurt. She had worn her loosest jeans and a shapeless gray sweater today, but it didn't matter. Nothing she did seemed to matter.

And it's all Will's fault, she reminded herself.

She hurried into class, head lowered, and slid into her seat as unobtrusively as possible. Her heart was pounding. Will was in this class. Any second he would walk into the room.

Jessica slid down lower in her seat. There was no escaping him.

Will entered the room just before the second bell, and she fixed him with a withering glare. This time, no matter what he said, she was not going to respond. Not one word.

As Will approached, she made sure her face betrayed no expression, but under her desk she was gripping her pencil so hard, she thought it would break. He was there. Right next to her. He was slowing down. Just being so close to him caused her skin to tingle with a mixture of revulsion and excitement. She was making herself sick.

And then he walked by.

Jessica slowly let the air out of her lungs as Will settled into his seat. She waited for him to turn and glance at her. Nothing. She frowned and started covering her paper with angry doodles.

But you told him to leave you alone, she thought. For once he was actually doing what she wanted.

So why did she suddenly feel so disappointed?

Angel finished toweling himself off and pulled on a clean pair of pants. It had taken fifteen minutes to scrub off the last trace of grime from the garage, but he finally felt clean. Now he had three hours of freedom before his shift at the Riot. It wasn't much, but it was his only downtime all day. Too bad Tia was stuck in cheerleading practice.

He pulled on a jacket and headed for his car. It was a beautiful fall day. A few clouds were the only sign of yesterday's downpour. The rain had left the air smelling cleaner than it had in weeks.

It was way too nice a day to be inside. Besides, if he spent one more second around his dad, he was going to crack a tooth from clenching his jaw. His dad was always hard to get along with, but now that money was getting tight around the shop, the guy had become impossible.

Angel hopped in his car and drove off, rolling down the window to let the breeze flow over him. It felt good to relax. He hadn't spoken to anyone about anything but cars all day. He decided to swing by Conner's house. Whether the guy liked it or not, Angel was concerned about him. Maybe he could convince Conner to get out of the house and lighten up.

Conner had been in a foul mood ever since that fight with Elizabeth. Angel didn't know exactly what had gone down, but he knew that Elizabeth had ended up moving out of Conner's house and that Conner was acting more bizarre than ever. One minute he was *über*bitter, and the next he was dragging people out for guys' nights at the track. It was like a bad split-personality movie on that women's cable channel.

Angel pulled into Conner's driveway, jogged up the walk, and rang the bell. It took Conner a while to get to the door. He had dark circles under his eyes, and he actually frowned when he saw Angel.

"Hey," Conner said flatly.

"Hey, man," Angel responded, trying not to let Conner's attitude get to him. "I was thinking of heading over to the track. Tia's at practice, and I thought it might be cool to get out for a while."

"The track, huh?" Conner asked. "So now you're a regular?"

"Hey, I've only gone once. But we didn't even make it out of the lounge. I want to see the horses this time. And I feel like being outside after working under cars all day. C'mon, man."

"No, thanks. It was pretty cool the other night, but I don't feel the need to go back." Conner paused and stared at a point past Angel's shoulder. "It's depressing, seeing all those guys who get sucked in and practically live there."

"All right, forget the track," Angel said. "What do you feel like doing?"

Conner scowled. "My mom's been sick. I told her I'd stay home." Angel heard someone moving around inside. Conner glanced over his shoulder and quickly stepped outside, shutting the door behind him.

"Everything all right, man?" Angel asked, rubbing his hands together slowly.

"Yeah. Fine," Conner answered, crossing his arms over his chest.

Angel blew out a short breath and decided to cut his losses. Conner obviously wasn't in party-guy mode today.

"All right, then," he said. "I guess I'll just go over there by myself. Grab a hot dog or something."

"It's your life." Conner shrugged.

"Yeah. Well, if there's a horse named Misanthrope, I'll put two dollars on him for you," Angel said with a laugh, trying to bring some levity into the conversation.

"Oh, so you're betting now? A minute ago you were just watching." Conner leaned against the door and smirked at him.

"Hey, I'm still three hundred up from last time. Even if I lose, I'll still have more than when I started." Angel hadn't really thought about it before, but he suddenly realized he was excited to see if his lucky streak would continue.

"It's your money," Conner said. "What are you doing tomorrow night?"

"I'm going out with Tia. It's our anniversary," Angel said. "You want to do something Friday instead?"

Conner nodded. "Yeah. That's cool."

Angel slapped hands with Conner and started to walk away, but he paused when he realized Conner hadn't gone back inside yet. He turned and looked at his friend. Conner glanced away.

"What's up, man?" Angel asked, pulling his keys out of his pocket.

Conner sighed noisily and adjusted his arms, wrapping them a little tighter around his gray T-shirt. "Just don't go too crazy at the track," he said. "Bad things happen there. I've seen it."

Angel almost laughed at Conner's melodramatic tone. "Don't worry," Angel said as he climbed into his car. "I'm fine."

Conner walked back inside as Angel revved the engine. He shook his head and laughed. What was the big deal anyway? He wasn't going to do anything stupid. How could he? He wouldn't even be gambling with his own money. If he lost, he was no worse off than when he started. But if he won . . . who knew how much he might come home with?

Conner McDermott

I had a bad feeling about Liz moving in from the beginning. And you know what? I was right. It just goes to show, if you have a bad feeling about something, listen to it.

But no, I let myself get distracted by her blond hair, her smooth skin, her innocent eyes. I let my guard down. I was seduced by her optimism, her naive faith that people are good and everything always turns out all right.

Well, in her world everything may be happiness and sunshine, but not in mine.

In my world your mother gets in drunken arguments with potted plants in the bars of ritzy country clubs—and that's the parent who cared enough to stick around.

CHAPTER
Brave New World
4

Ken opened the school library door and peered in. He'd only been inside the library a few times in his life, and whenever he showed his face, he half expected someone to ask what he was doing there. Nobody even looked up.

It was eerily calm inside. Rows of identical, sturdy wooden tables, mostly empty, stretched to the far wall, and shafts of light from the afternoon sun lit particles of dust that were floating lazily in the air. A few kids sat alone, studying. Outside, his old teammates were yelling and smacking into one another on the football field, but in here all that seemed very far away. He walked quietly through the vast room, his footsteps echoing off the high ceiling, and sat down at a table near the window.

It was weird being in school after classes let out. The halls were strangely quiet. Like almost everyone else, he was usually out of the building the second the last bell rang. Studying in the library after school was like entering a whole new world. A world peopled by a handful of nerds scribbling away in notebooks or typing on laptop computers. Well, he was one of them now.

He opened Maria's history notebook and flipped through it. He had never seen such neat handwriting. Each page was dated at the top, and her notes were all organized under headings and subheadings with letters and roman numerals. He dimly remembered some teacher explaining "outline form" years ago, but he hadn't realized anyone actually used it to take notes. Could she really have written all this down while the teacher was lecturing? It was all he could do to understand what the teacher was saying, much less write it down, but Maria had managed to organize it all into topics and subtopics. No wonder those A-student types looked so intent in class all the time.

He read on, feeling like he was soaking up weeks of classes in less than an hour. He was so absorbed that when someone tapped him on the shoulder, he almost fell out of his chair.

"Hey, brainiac." He looked up to find Maria hovering over him. "How's it going?"

"Uh, I just got here," he said, feeling an inexplicable blush rise to his cheeks. It was weird, but she looked really pretty standing there looking down at him. Her hair was flopping forward over her headband, and the way it framed her face made him think of one of those fashion-magazine models.

Maria smiled slightly and slid into the chair across from him. "I just wanted to stop by and say hi before I went to the *Oracle* meeting. See if everything in there made sense." She gestured at her notebook.

Ken scoffed. "Are you kidding? This thing is pure gold."

"What do you mean?" Maria asked, glancing at the pages as he flipped through them.

"I always wondered how you could remember every little thing the teacher said for a whole semester," Ken said, shifting in his seat. "I mean, there would be all these questions on the final exam, and I would be, like, who can remember all this stuff? But if you take notes like this . . ."

Maria rolled her eyes, but she was grinning. "Everybody takes notes, Ken. It's no big deal."

"Not like these." Ken slumped back in his chair. "I mean, I write stuff down, but I can barely read it a week later, and half the time I don't know what I was talking about."

"So, what do you do before a test?" Maria asked, her brow knitting.

"I don't know . . . flip through the book, try to remember stuff. Not that it ever did me much good. You can't read a whole book the night before the test."

"My friend, you need some *serious* help." Maria shook her head slightly.

Ken smiled and pushed a shock of blond hair out of his eyes. "I know," he said. "But that's what I have you for, right?"

"Hey! I didn't sign on to be your tutor," Maria whispered, pushing back in her seat. "You want this girl to teach you the ropes, you'd better come up with some cash."

Ken laughed. "Nah. You'll do it 'cause you like me." The second the words were out of his mouth, he wanted to gobble them back. He stared at the wooden tabletop, hoping she might have gone temporarily deaf.

"I don't know if I'd say I *like* you," Maria said finally. "But you're tolerable."

"Great. Thanks a lot," Ken answered, sounding offended but feeling relieved.

"So, I'd better take off." Maria stood. "I'll see you at your house tonight."

"Yeah," Ken said.

He looked down at the notebook as Maria walked away, but as soon as her back was safely to him, he watched her walk to the door. Then he stared after her moments after she'd gone.

What's wrong with me? Ken thought suddenly, sitting up straight and taking a deep breath. He felt like he'd just been in a trance. And the last thing he needed right now was to go all foggy. He pulled

Maria's notebook to him and flipped it open. If he was going to pull his weight tonight and not completely embarrass himself, he had a lot of work ahead of him.

"Heads up!"

Will looked up to see a football whistling right toward his face. He managed to get his hands up in time to keep from losing an eye. Todd Wilkins was standing ten yards downfield, laughing.

"Nice catch," Todd called. He started jogging away, looking over his shoulder for Will to throw him a pass.

Will reared back and fired. Todd took off at full speed, glanced up at the ball, then stopped. It was going way over his head. Will laughed as Todd stopped and shook his head at him. It wasn't until someone called, "Nice pass!" from far down the field that Todd spun and saw Jake Collins carrying the football into the end zone a good forty yards away.

"Nice one, Simmons," Todd said, jogging over. "With a little practice, you might just have a future." He slapped Will on the back.

Will unsnapped his chin strap and pulled off his helmet. His hair was plastered to his forehead and soaked with sweat, and when he ran his hands through his hair, he had to wipe them on his jersey. The football players trudged off the muddy field toward the locker room. Even after a hard, two-hour practice Will's hands were still itching to grab a football and fling it. He was still flying high from the prepractice meeting. After a few weeks of pointless stalling and mulling it over, Coach Riley had finally named Will captain.

They kicked the mud off their cleats outside the locker-room door. Once inside, Will sank onto the worn wooden bench in front of his locker. He felt like his whole body was sighing in relief and realized it was actually a good thing he hadn't extended practice any longer.

Todd pulled off his shoulder pads and damp T-shirt, then stretched, his arms above his head. "Not a bad practice," he said.

Will nodded. "I'm glad I'm playing on this team, not against it." He knew that if he were back at El Carro High, SVH would pose a serious threat. He didn't mind playing with the best of both teams.

Other players were streaming into the locker room, and the cement walls echoed with the sound of scuffling and clanging doors. Soon the showers started blasting in the next room, filling the echoing chamber with white noise.

"Now that you're captain," Todd said, glancing over his shoulder, "there's something I wanted to talk to you about."

Will stopped untying his shoe and straightened his back with a crack. "What's up?"

"Did you guys do a kidnap at your school?" Todd asked.

"What's a kidnap?" Will asked.

"We do it every year," Todd said, plopping down next to Will on the bench. "Early one Saturday morning everyone on the football team and the cheerleading squad gets woken up and dragged out of bed. You have to get in the car without a shower or changing your clothes or anything, and then everyone goes out for breakfast."

"Sounds like torture," Will said.

Todd laughed. "I know. But it's pretty cool to see the girls in their nightgowns."

Will raised his eyebrows. "The cheerleaders?"

"Yeah. They're all there in their pajamas or whatever they sleep in, and their hair's all a mess." Todd scratched his head, mussing his own curly hair. "They hate it. It's pretty funny."

Will laughed. "No doubt," he said, imagining the tantrum Melissa would throw if she had to leave the house with zit cream on. Then his mind flashed on a picture of Jessica in a skimpy nightgown, and he blushed. He had to shake his head to clear the thought.

Todd tossed his cleats into his locker with a bang. "The thing is, nobody can know when it's going to happen, or that ruins it. The only people who know are the people who organize it—the captain of the cheerleading team and the captain of the football team." He looked at Will, waiting for the news to sink in.

"Hold it," Will said with a smirk. "You want me to *run* this thing? I've never even been to one! Can't you do it?"

"It's not my responsibility, man," Todd said. He laughed and punched Will's shoulder. "You've only been captain two hours, and you're wimping out already?"

"I'm serious. Tia doesn't know anything about this either," Will said. "How are we supposed to organize it? Wait. Who did it last year?"

"Ken and Jessica."

Will was suddenly very aware of his pulse. "Jessica Wakefield?" His face was flushed again. He grabbed a towel and pretended to wipe the sweat off his forehead.

"If you want help, you'd probably be better off talking to Ken," Todd said.

"Why? The guy hates me," Will said, knowing it wasn't true. Ken just didn't want to have anything to do with the team.

"I don't know, Simmons," Todd said, his brown eyes narrowed. "You and Jessica? Probably not the best idea."

Will turned to his locker and started pulling out his shower stuff. Where did Todd get off, giving him advice?

"I'll handle it," he said evenly, slamming his locker with his foot.

"Cool," Todd said with a shrug.

Will took a deep breath and headed for the showers, feeling his irritation washed away by excitement over the idea of getting together with Jessica. This was the answer to his prayers. Jessica would have to talk to him now.

And after that, anything could happen.

Angel leaned forward, watching intently as the horses rounded the final stretch. It was much nicer outside. Why would anyone spend the whole evening in the smoke-filled clubhouse, watching the races on TV, when they could sit in the bleachers and get up close and personal with the horses?

The only problem was, it was harder to follow what was happening. Where was horse number four? He had lost sight of him when they had all bunched together in the turn.

Suddenly a light brown horse burst out of the pack and made a charge for the lead. Two other horses kept pace, and the rest dropped back. Running third was horse number four, Cupid.

When Angel had seen the name, he had instantly decided to bet on him. And although he'd planned to bet only five dollars, he had impulsively added another twenty at the last minute. With his and Tia's anniversary coming up, a horse named Cupid had to be good luck.

As they neared the finish line, the three lead horses were running neck and neck. Angel rose to his feet, along with the rest of the crowd. Everyone around him was yelling like crazy, but Angel just clenched his fists and murmured under his breath, "Come on, Cupid. Come on, boy."

With a final burst of speed Cupid lunged forward and crossed the finish line, ahead by a nose. Angel raised both fists in the air triumphantly. Around him most of the crowd slumped back into their seats. But a few others remained standing, clapping and cheering. Angel caught the eye of a laughing man to his left and grinned.

Cupid had been an eight-to-one long shot. Angel's twenty-five-dollar bet was now worth two hundred bucks. He felt the slick ticket in his pocket proudly. Next to it was a thick stack of bills from his previous winnings. He'd never felt so free in his life.

On his way to the window to cash in his ticket, Angel saw a pay phone out of the corner of his eye. He almost walked past it, then stopped. He knew exactly what he should do with that money.

He dialed Tia's number. She answered on the fourth ring.

"Hey, baby!" she said happily. "What's up?"

"I'm calling about our anniversary," he said.

"I've been thinking about that," Tia said. "I've got a great idea. Remember that movie we saw on our first date? I was thinking we could rent it, and we could get the exact same pizza we ate that night—pepperoni, mushroom, and olives from Giordi's. We can do everything the same—except the good-night kiss can last longer. Maybe an extra hour or two? What do you say?"

"I've got a better idea," Angel said, dodging a racing form as it blew by. "But it's a surprise."

"What do you mean? Don't I get to help decide?"

"Nope." Angel shifted his weight to his other foot, struggling to contain his excitement. "Just be ready at seven o'clock. And wear your best dress."

"Ooh, I'm intrigued," Tia said. "Okay. I'll be ready at seven."

"Cool," Angel said with a grin. "I can't wait."

"Me neither," Tia responded. "Where are you anyway? It sounds like you're on the street somewhere."

Angel hunched over to shield the receiver from the crowd. "I gotta run, or I'll be late for work. See you, baby. I love you." He hung up the phone and fingered the wad of bills in his pocket one more time. He couldn't remember the last time he had felt this good.

As Maria rang the doorbell at Ken's house, she marveled at how things had changed since last year. Here she was, Miss Boring A Student, hanging out with the former football captain and social ringleader of Sweet Valley High. No one would have believed this a year ago. *She* wouldn't have believed this a year ago.

The door opened, and Ken greeted Maria with his perfect smile. "Hey," he said. "Come on in."

"Thanks," Maria said, shrugging out of her jacket as she followed him into a comfortable living room. It was filled with overstuffed furniture arranged around a gigantic TV. The house had a cozy, lived-in look. A few copies of *Sports Illustrated* lay on a coffee table. The walls were covered with pictures of Ken in uniform. A display case filled with Ken's athletic trophies and some older ones that must have been his father's stood in the corner. The wall-to-wall carpet was a nondescript beige color, but it was thick and soft. She thought of her own living room, with its grand piano, Persian rugs, and austere wood surfaces. Ken's house made hers seem cold and stuffy in comparison.

"You want a soda or anything?" Ken asked. "I've been dosing on sugar and caffeine to get ready." He held up an empty cola can and grinned.

"Sure. I could use some of both," Maria said. "Just don't try to give me that diet stuff."

"Ooh, I'm impressed," he said. "Follow me." He led her through the dining room, where the newspaper was spread across the table. It was open to the sports section.

Ken took a soda from the refrigerator and poured it into a tall glass. "Your notes are upstairs," he said.

"Where are your parents?" Maria asked.

"My mom lives in Florida with my stepdad, and my dad's not home from work yet," Ken said, handing her the drink.

"What's your dad do?" Maria asked, taking a sip.

"Shockingly enough, he's a sportswriter for the *Sweet Valley Tribune*," Ken said with a sardonic smile. "He's covering a soccer game at SVU tonight."

"Cool," Maria said as they climbed the stairs to Ken's room. "Yeah. At least it keeps him out of the house," Ken answered. Walking behind him, Maria raised her eyebrows at his last comment but said nothing. She knew what it was like to need serious nonparental time.

Ken's room was exactly what Maria had expected. The walls were decorated with posters commemorating the last five Super Bowls, and his bed was covered by a brown plaid comforter. To her surprise, however, there was also a book lying open on his bed. She picked it up and leafed through it. It was a book of poems.

"Robert Frost's *You Come Too*?" she said, puzzled. "Was this a gift from Olivia?"

Ken blinked rapidly. "She told me about it." He shrugged. "I got it after she died." He gingerly removed the book from her hand, and Maria suddenly felt like she had done something wrong.

"So, do you want to start?" she asked, looking awkwardly around the room.

"Yeah." Ken laid the book on his desk and sat down. "Your notebook was really helpful, by the way. Can you show me how to take notes like that?" He handed her the notebook.

Maria's brow wrinkled, and she looked in his eyes to see if he was mocking her. Apparently not.

"Sure, if you want," she said. "But let's get going on our project first." She sat on the edge of the bed and pulled out her organizer. "We should start by making a schedule. Let's see, we have four weeks left. That gives us a couple of weeks to do the research, then a week to write first drafts, then we'll have a week to combine and edit our sections. Does that sound good?"

He shrugged. "Whatever," he said. "Just tell me what I have to do, and I'll do it."

"Okay, let's start blocking out the schedule," Maria said. "Can I see your planner?"

Ken looked at her blankly. "I don't have one."

"You're kidding," Maria said.

"Nope," Ken said. "All I've got is that." He pointed at a calendar hanging on the wall, featuring a model in a swimsuit.

Maria squinted at it. "That's from last year!"

"Can't seem to part with her, though," Ken said with a sly smile.

Maria whacked his arm with her leather planner. "Loser," she said, blushing. "How do you plan your time?"

Ken frowned and scratched the back of his head. "What's to plan? School. Used to have practice, but now that's out. Then I do landscaping on weekends, but it's always the same place, same time."

"But what about schoolwork?" Maria asked. "How do you know when your assignments are due?"

"I just write down homework assignments in my notebook. The teachers always remind you about that stuff in class anyway."

Maria shook her head. "Wow, I could never handle that. I'd freak if I found out I left something until the last minute."

Ken laughed. "You're so abnormal."

Maria felt her face grow hot, but for some unknown reason, she was smiling. "What's that supposed to mean?"

"It means no self-respecting teenager should be this responsible," Ken said, grabbing her planner from her. He flipped through the well-worn pages and then just let it fall open. "I don't believe it," Ken said, his eyes running over one of Maria's daily "to do" lists. "You write down when you need to change the kitty litter?"

Maria laughed and grabbed the book back. "Yeah? Well, I don't think any self-respecting teenager should be this *ir*responsible," she said, leaning over and snatching the calendar off the wall.

"When you're quarterback of the football team, most teachers are pretty cool about giving you extensions," Ken said, grabbing the calendar back from her. He placed it on the desk next to the poetry book and just stared at it for a moment. "I guess that's not going to work anymore, is it?"

A tense silence filled the air, and Maria felt herself gripping his bedspread. Sometimes Ken was so hard to read. One minute he was joking, and the next he was off in his own little world. But at that moment Maria knew he was thinking about his old life. About Olivia and football and how perfect things used to be. She felt a little lump forming in her throat and had to nip her sentimentality in the bud.

"You know what we should do? We should go shopping tomorrow and get you one of these," she said, holding up her planner again.

Ken sighed. "It's not like I have anything else to do," he said. "Might as well make the complete crossover into the land of the dorks." He gave her a small smile.

"Very funny," Maria said, patting him hard on the shoulder. "Let me just make sure." She flipped through her planner and for once grinned at the emptiness that greeted her under the heading 4 P.M.–8 P.M. "Nope. No sign of a social life here. Looks like you're in luck."

Elizabeth Wakefield

From: lizw@cal.rr.com
To: jess1@cal.rr.com
Time: 3:58 P.M.
Subject: HOJ

  Hi, Jess. I can't believe I'm
e-mailing you. But I know you'll check
your e-mail the second you get home. I
was really looking forward to hanging
out with you last night—but I
understand why you wanted to see
Jeremy. Anyway, can we talk later? I'm
at the <u>Oracle</u> for another half hour or
so, but maybe we could go to House of
Java. I just need to talk.
                        Later.
                        Liz

Jessica Wakefield

To: lizw@cal.rr.com
From: jess1@cal.rr.com
Time: 4:26 P.M.
Subject: Re: HOJ

Hey!
I'm sorry that I can't meet you later. I'm leaving for work in half an hour. I know we were supposed to hang out last night, but I really just needed to chill with Jeremy after that whole scene with Will. I really want to talk to you. I feel like I've hardly seen you in days. Save tomorrow night, okay? I'll see you then.

Jess

Ken Matthews

Dear Olivia:

  You know I was never much of a writer, but I've been thinking about you a lot, and I really wanted to talk to you.

  After you died, I felt so guilty, I didn't feel like I deserved to live. I thought if I was happy, I would be betraying your memory. So I didn't even try.

  But now that I've blown off the team, school, and my future, whenever I think of you, I _really_ feel guilty. I know you'd hate to see me throwing my life away like this.

  So I've been trying harder to keep going. But what I wanted to talk to you about is, I've been hanging around with Maria Slater a lot lately.

  The thing is, I think it's really helping me. I'd pretty much given up on the future. But her future still means a lot to her, so I've been thinking about mine too. Who knows? Maybe I'll actually have one. A future, I mean. I'll keep you posted.

Love, Ken

CHAPTER
Bad Habit
5

Jessica set down her forkful of filet mignon. The gourmet meal provided by the Fowlers' chef had been completely wasted on her. She couldn't have said whether the fresh fruit rémoulade had contained kiwis, capers, or ketchup. The strained atmosphere around the dinner table wasn't helping her appetite.

After weeks of living together uncomfortably under one roof, the Fowlers and the Wakefields had simply run out of things to talk about. And Lila still treated Jessica like she had an infectious disease. Elizabeth, who normally at least tried to keep things polite, had said a total of about three words since she moved back after her run-in with Conner. It was not the ideal recipe for dinnertime chat.

"So, how's the new fashion editor turning out, Liz?" Lila said out of the blue.

Jessica almost spit out her water, but Elizabeth didn't even look up. "Fine," she said, and continued to push her peas listlessly around her plate with her fork.

"I'm not surprised. Since she got the job over the

person who came up with the idea, she must be a fashion genius. Though you sure wouldn't have known it from that jumper she was wearing today. I guess last year's fashions are making a comeback, and she's the only one who's heard about it."

"Lila!" her mother said. Lila rolled her eyes, and the uncomfortable silence resumed.

Mrs. Wakefield cleared her throat. "Girls—everyone—your father and I received some very good news today," she said with a forced smile.

Neither Elizabeth nor Jessica answered. Finally Mrs. Fowler filled the awkward silence. "That's wonderful. I'm sure we'd all love to hear some good news."

"Well, Grace . . . George," Mrs. Wakefield said, glancing at the Fowlers. "I can't thank you enough for letting us stay with you while our house is being rebuilt. But I think the girls will be glad to hear that I spoke with our contractor today, and he said our new house is almost ready." She beamed at Jessica and Elizabeth. "We'll be able to move in about two weeks!"

Jessica felt like the air had been let back into the room and she could suddenly breathe again. She imagined herself back in her own room, looking out the window at the old familiar trees on her block, and an ache in her heart she hadn't even realized was there started to loosen. She sat up straight in her chair. "Mrs. Fowler, may I please be excused?"

Mrs. Fowler laughed. "Go ahead. I know you're excited. . . ."

Jessica didn't hear her finish because she had already dashed halfway up the stairs.

Finally! The next two weeks couldn't pass fast enough.

Jessica pulled open the huge closet that contained piles of things she had salvaged from her room after the quake. She'd never bothered to sort through a lot of it, but all she wanted to do now was get packing—even if she wouldn't actually get to leave for two weeks.

She picked up the phone and called Jeremy. "Is this my manly-man, football-player boyfriend?" she asked.

"Maybe. Depends on who's calling," Jeremy said.

Jessica laughed. "You won't believe this. I'm moving back home! If you're not too tired from work, I was wondering if you wanted to come over and help me carry stuff."

"I don't believe it. Someone who appreciates me for more than just my brain," Jeremy joked.

"Brain?" Jessica asked. "I wasn't aware you actually had one of those."

"Yeah, yeah, yeah," Jeremy said. "What's with the excitement? You're not moving tonight, are you?"

Jessica rolled her eyes. "No. I just want to get started. I have a lot to get rid of and—"

"Oh, I get it," Jeremy said. "You want me to help

clean your room. Why didn't you just tell me you were lazy?"

"Jeremy—"

He laughed, cutting her off. "I'll be right over."

Jessica hung up the phone and turned to find Elizabeth standing in her doorway.

"Who were you calling?" Elizabeth asked, her eyes dull.

That was when Jessica realized she was supposed to hang out with Elizabeth.

"Jeremy," Jessica said, guilt settling in on her shoulders. "I could call back and cancel," she said, reaching for the phone.

"Don't bother. I know Jeremy will be a lot better company than me," Elizabeth said. "I've got . . . stuff to do anyway."

"You can hang out with us," Jessica suggested.

Elizabeth snorted a laugh. "Yeah. That sounds like fun," she said sarcastically.

Jessica blinked, stung as Elizabeth turned and walked slowly down the hall.

"We'll do something tomorrow, okay?" Jessica called after her. Her sister's fatalism just made it worse. She was too depressed to even stand up for herself.

Jessica promised herself she would spend some time with Elizabeth the next day. She couldn't let her sister walk around in this morose state much longer.

*   *   *

"I can't believe how huge this place is," Ken said. He followed Maria to the checkout counter, pushing their shopping cart ahead of him. "I never knew half this stuff even existed."

"What do you mean?" Maria asked. "You've never been to an office-supply store before?"

"No. I would always get my stuff from the drugstore." He opened his new, black planner gingerly, as if it had just dropped from a UFO, then placed it back in the cart. "Look at all this stuff—safari-colored Post-it notes, ergo-something mouse pads, color-coded paper clips." He unloaded the contents of their cart onto the counter. "This place is like another planet. I bet I'm the first football player who ever set foot in here."

"Hi, Maria," the cashier said with a smile. "Did you get your printer working again?"

"Yeah. It turned out all it needed was some new toner. I don't know how it got empty so quick. I must have been using it more than I realized."

The clerk lowered her voice. "I'm not supposed to tell you this, but there's going to be a sale on toner next week, if you want to stock up. I know how fast you go through that stuff."

"Thanks, Tina," Maria said, handing her a credit card.

On the way out, Maria gave the clerk a friendly wave, and Ken shook his head, smiling. "You must really be a regular here. Do *all* the clerks know your name?"

"Come on. Tina lives on my block," Maria said. "I'm not *that* bad."

Ken laughed. "There was a guy at Sports Expert who used to know my name, shoe size, and hat size, so it's all good."

They reached Ken's car, and Maria reached for the door handle, then paused. "You think I'm a total nerd, don't you?" she said.

Ken's heart took an unexpected nosedive. She was trying to be lighthearted, but the tone of her voice betrayed her. "No," he said slowly. "I was just kidding."

"I know," Maria said, watching as he popped the lock and opened the back door to put the bag inside. "But sometimes I think that everyone just writes me off. Like I do well in school, so I must just be uncool or whatever."

Ken shut the door and leaned on top of the car, leveling her with a stare. Funny. He had never felt comfortable looking anyone in the eye, but with Maria he had no problem.

"You're not uncool," he said. "Anyone who thinks that just doesn't know you."

Maria managed a small smile, and Ken let out a breath of relief. She opened the door and slid into the passenger seat. Ken plopped down next to her and noticed she was fiddling with the white string that was hanging from a hole in her jeans. He wanted to try to make her more comfortable, but he didn't know what else to say.

He started the engine.

"You know," Maria said, staring at her fingers as they pulled at the string. "When I met Conner, it was just . . . nice. . . ." She looked up and stared through the windshield. "Like, here was this cool guy, and he picked me. Me."

Ken just watched her profile, his heart pounding. This line of conversation was making him tense, but he didn't want to stop her. She obviously wanted to talk about this.

"I felt, like, I don't know, different." She finally turned to look at him, and from reflex Ken looked away. He wasn't sure what she would be able to read in his expression. Out of the corner of his eye he saw her shift in her seat and look out the passenger-side window. "It doesn't matter," she said quietly.

Ken just sat there, listening to the motor idle, feeling the sweat coating his palms. He had to say something. *Anything*. But what was he supposed to say? *I'm sorry things didn't work out between you and Conner?* He couldn't say that. It wasn't remotely true.

"Maria . . ."

She turned to look at him, her eyebrows raised.

"Do you have to go home right away?" Ken asked.

"Well, I do have a lot of homework—" She stopped. "No, I don't. Why?"

"Because I was thinking. . . ." He wiped his palms

on his jeans and hoped she didn't notice the little stains they left there. "Do you want to get something to eat?"

The tension slowly faded from Maria's face. "Yeah," she said. "It would be nice to just relax for a while."

Ken smiled, and Maria grinned back, momentarily causing him to forget what he was supposed to be doing. Then he snapped out of it and put the car in gear as Maria leaned over and cranked up the radio. He had to concentrate on keeping his eyes on the road and off Maria.

What am I doing? Ken wondered. A couple of weeks ago he would have gotten up and walked away if someone sat down next to him in the lunchroom. Now he had just asked a girl out to dinner. And the weirdest thing was, he was actually looking forward to it.

Angel straightened his tie and admired himself in the mirror. Tia loved this suit. And when she saw where he was taking her, she was going to flip out. He felt the thick wad of bills in his jacket pocket and smiled. *Thank you, horses,* he thought. *And the jockeys too. Let's not forget the jockeys.* He'd have to have a drink in their honor.

"Where are you going, dressed up like that?" his father demanded as soon as Angel set foot in the living room. Mr. Desmond was sitting in his recliner in black jeans and a clean white T-shirt, watching the news.

Angel gritted his teeth. This had to be the one night his father decided to hang in the living room instead of upstairs in the den.

"Look at you," Mr. Desmond continued. "I didn't have a suit when I was your age. The first time I wore a suit was the day I married your mother. And that wasn't until I owned my own shop and was ready to support a family. You had to earn things back then." He lifted a muscular arm to mute the TV with the remote control. "What's so important you have to wear a suit on a weeknight?"

"It's Tia's and my anniversary. We're going out to dinner," Angel said, keeping his voice neutral.

"I hope you're not spending all your college money on that girl," his father said. "I still can't believe you turned down a scholarship to Stanford University so you wouldn't have to leave your girlfriend."

"I didn't turn it down," Angel said. "I deferred. There's a difference."

His father shook his head. "You could be at Stanford this very minute, but no, you'd rather clean tables in some nightclub, then go out and fritter away your salary on a girl."

Angel felt the familiar sensation of all the blood rushing to his face, but he held his tongue.

"You don't know what it means to work for a living." Mr. Desmond held up his hand, showing Angel

71

his callused fingers. "When I was your age, I was working full-time, and I haven't stopped since. I only wish you appreciated the opportunity you're being given."

Angel's back was rigid. "I wasn't *given* that opportunity; I *earned* it," he said. He clenched his fists, trying to stay calm. "You don't think I had to work my butt off to get into Stanford?" His father opened his mouth, but before he could tell Angel not to talk back to him, Angel cut him off. "Look, I *know* what I'm doing. I'm sorry you didn't get to go to college, but that's not my fault. I wish you'd just get off my back." With that, he stalked out, slamming the door behind him.

Will reached for the telephone, then stopped and tucked his hands under his arms. He had to handle this just right. This kidnap thing could be the perfect opportunity to get together with Jessica if he played it right.

He could say he was busy during the week, then suggest they meet on Friday night. That way, when they were done talking about the kidnap, the evening could sort of blur into a date. Perfect.

Then the doorbell rang.

Tense, Will headed for the entryway, prepared to tell whoever it was to just go away. But when he opened the door, his blood froze.

"Hi, Will. Can I come in?"

Melissa stepped past him into the living room.

"Of course," he said woodenly. He suddenly seemed to be having a hard time breathing.

She stood in the middle of the room and crossed her arms protectively over her chest.

"So, what's up?" Will said, shoving his hands into the pockets of his chinos.

"Nothing," Melissa said flatly.

Then why are you here? Will wanted to shout.

"All right, it's not nothing," Melissa said, as if responding to his thought. She crossed the distance between them and took one hand in hers, wrapping her fingers between his. Will felt his arm go heavy, and he didn't allow his hand to respond to her touch. But he didn't draw away either. He was too stunned.

"I miss you," she said, staring at their hands. Then she turned her clear blue eyes up and gazed into his face. "I miss you so much."

"Melissa—"

Suddenly her mouth was on his and she was pressing her lips firmly against his own. Will recoiled and pulled his hand out of her grasp. He fought the urge to wipe his mouth with the back of his hand.

"What are you doing?" he demanded.

Melissa narrowed her eyes at him. "I was just trying to give you another chance," she said, crossing her arms again. "Before you go and make an idiot out of yourself with Jessica Wakefield." As she said

Jessica's name, tears sprang to Melissa's eyes, but they didn't fall. "I know what you're doing, Will, but it's not going to work."

Now it was Will's turn to narrow his eyes. "What are you talking about?"

"Think about it!" Melissa said, throwing up her arms as if there was some obvious truth he was completely missing. "The girl has a boyfriend. And not only that, he's good-looking, rich, popular . . . and he didn't spend the first few weeks of school spreading rumors about her."

Will pulled back as if he'd been slapped. "That was you, not me!" he shouted.

"But you didn't speak up, did you? You didn't defend her." She leaned closer, and he felt like a fly pinned to the wall. "And where did the guys get the idea that she'd slept with Matt Wells? You two came up with that little piece of locker-room bragging on your own."

Will looked away.

"Anyway, most of what we said was *true*. She really *has* gone out with almost everyone on the football team." She stared into his eyes, and he felt himself weakening.

Melissa turned away for a moment, and Will told himself to get rid of her. He told himself to just walk over to the front door and usher her out of his life. But for some reason, he couldn't do that to her—as much as her presence irritated him, he still felt the need to protect her. It was like a bad habit.

When she turned around again, her expression was all pity, which only raised his ire all the more.

"It's not gonna happen, Will," she said in a soothing voice. "She's never going to choose you over Jeremy Aames." His jaw clenched and he tried to stare back at her defiantly, but her steady gaze forced him to look away. "And you know it," she said. "How are you going to feel when she's walking around school bragging about what an idiot you made of yourself over her?"

"That's not going to happen, Melissa," he said forcefully, training his eyes on hers once more.

She shrugged casually. "What makes you so sure?"

Don't do it, man, he told himself. *Don't let her get to you.* But he couldn't resist. She was so cocky and sure of herself. Sure, he was playing the simpering fool. He couldn't take it anymore. "Because I'm going out with her this Friday," he said.

For a split second Melissa's calm exterior cracked and her mouth fell open. But just as quickly, she snapped it shut again.

Will eyed her warily. She had to know he was lying. She *always* knew when he was lying.

"I should have known," she said finally. She actually laughed. "Of course she's cheating on her boyfriend. What did I expect?"

She stormed past him into the entryway, and Will

let out a breath he hadn't even realized he was holding. He turned just as she placed her hand on the doorknob. But of course, she couldn't go away without getting in one last word.

"If you want to be the flavor of the month for the school slut, that's fine," she spat. Then she looked him directly in the eye. "I'm done here."

Before Will could even register that she actually meant what she'd just said, she slammed the door behind her.

Angel Desmond

When I was in second grade, my teacher told us the story of George Washington and the cherry tree. I thought and thought about it, but I couldn't understand why George didn't get in trouble for chopping it down. Finally I asked my mom. She explained that although little George had done something bad, the important thing was that he told the truth. (I never did find out why he chopped down the tree.)

Later that week I was riding my new bike in the yard and I knocked

over my mother's favorite rosebush.
She had been fussing over it for years,
but I snapped it right over with my
front wheel and killed it. To my
amazement, my parents blamed it on
the neighbor's dog.

My mom got over it, but three
days later I still hadn't. I kept
thinking of George and the tree.
Finally I decided that if I confessed,
they would be so impressed by my
telling the truth that I wouldn't get
punished. On Saturday morning,
over my bowl of Lucky Charms, I
told them what happened.

Apparently George's father was

nothing like mine. By the time my dad got through with me, I was wishing I'd been fed through the chipper with the rosebush.

CHAPTER
Monsters Under the Bed

6

"Jessica?" Jeremy dropped the heavy bag of clothes on the floor next to the bed.

"I'm in here," Jessica shouted from the walk-in closet.

Jeremy straightened up and stretched. "I got the bag up from the basement," he said, looking around at the random clothes strewn all over the room. It looked like a department store had exploded in her bedroom. "God, how much clothing do you have?"

"I know, it's insane," Jessica said, her voice muffled. "I hardly wear any of it anymore. That's why I want to give some of it away before we move."

"So what should I do now?" Jeremy asked, sitting on the edge of the bed. "Want me to sort through your lingerie?"

Jessica walked to the doorway of the closet and chucked a sweater at him, hitting him hard on the chest. Then she just disappeared again. Jeremy laughed and tossed the sweater over his shoulder onto the mattress.

"Why don't you see if there's anything under the

bed, Romeo?" Jessica called. "Maybe something will jump out and bite you."

"Funny." Jeremy sighed and hit the floor on his hands and knees. "A boyfriend's work is never done," he muttered to himself, pulling up the flowered dust ruffle. The foot-tall space was littered with shopping bags, magazines, and other random debris. Jeremy pulled out a plastic bag. Inside was a tangled mess of T-shirts and tank tops. He dumped the contents onto the bed next to another pile of stuff so that Jessica could go through it.

The next bag was heavier and clunkier. Inside were a couple of boxes and some envelopes. He opened a gold box about the size of a book, but it was empty. The second was a black velvet jewelry box. He popped it open, and a thick silver necklace slipped out and plopped into a pile on the plush carpet.

Jeremy picked it up and draped it over his fingers. Jessica didn't seem like the type to cast something this expensive aside. And it looked like a gift. What was it doing under the bed?

And who had given it to her?

Don't get paranoid, he thought, trying to control the impending wave of jealousy before it took over. It was probably just a present from some old boyfriend. It had nothing to do with him.

Jeremy's eyes fell on one of the envelopes, and his

heart skipped a beat. He quickly checked the closet and then picked up the envelope before his conscience got the better of him.

His hands were shaking as he read the card.

"You must remember this, a kiss is still a kiss,
A sigh is just a sigh."

Jeremy swallowed hard. Okay, so it wasn't from her parents. Feeling suddenly dizzy, he stuffed the note back in the bag. *I shouldn't be reading this,* he thought. *It's none of my business.*

Besides, it couldn't possibly be what it seemed. Jessica wouldn't lie to him about something like that. Summer boyfriend. That had to be it. Problem was, he sort of remembered Jessica saying she hadn't dated anyone since last spring. There had to be another explanation. Unfortunately he couldn't think of one right now. The important thing was not to jump to conclusions.

The closet door swung open, and he quickly shoved the bag back under the bed.

"There!" Jessica emerged, dragging a huge shopping bag behind her. "All of this stuff can go to the Salvation Army. Not bad, huh?" She was wearing a pair of running shorts and a white tank top, and her tan skin was gleaming with sweat. She wiped her hand over her forehead and grinned.

"Yeah. That's great," Jeremy said. He stood up,

moved away from the bed, and forced himself to smile back at her.

Jessica spread her arms and flopped backward onto the bed. "I can't believe I'm finally going to be free of this place!" she said. "I feel like I'm being released from prison!" She bounced up again and wrapped her arms around Jeremy, then kissed him on the cheek. "I feel like celebrating," she said, stretching her arms up over her head. "Let's go get some ice cream!"

Jeremy smiled weakly. "Sure. If you want," he mumbled, sticking his hands in the pockets of his jeans. She was radiant, and it was all too easy to imagine somebody falling in love with her and showering her with gifts.

He would give her jewelry too, if he could afford it.

"What's wrong?" Jessica asked, studying his face.

"Nothing," Jeremy said. He couldn't even talk to her about it because he shouldn't have been looking at her private stuff. But then again, she *had* asked him to clean up under the bed. Did that mean there was nothing to be suspicious about? Or did it mean she had *wanted* him to find it for some reason? Or was he just rapidly losing his mind?

Jeremy sank to the edge of the bed.

Jessica sat down next to him. "Are you okay?" she asked.

"Yeah. I guess I'm just tired." He smiled at her. Fortunately he'd had a lot of practice with false cheerfulness recently. But somehow this pit-of-the-stomach feeling was almost worse than being around his dad. It was newer—sharper. "If I'd known how much stuff you had, I would have rented a moving van on the way over."

"I know. It looks like we both worked up a sweat," she said, looking at his hairline.

Jeremy wiped his forehead with the back of his hand, knowing he wasn't sweating from physical labor. "You know what? Ice cream sounds good. Let's go."

Jessica grabbed him as he tried to stand and pulled him back down. She draped her arms around his neck. "Nope. First I get a kiss," she said.

Jeremy's stomach tightened as her lips touched his. He kissed her back as convincingly as he could, but when he closed his eyes, he immediately imagined her passionately embracing someone else. He pulled away abruptly and tried to smile.

"Sorry. That's all I can handle until I get fed," he joked, turning away so she couldn't see his face.

Jessica grabbed her purse from the top of her dresser. "Ready when you are," she said. "I'm buying since you helped me with all this." She held open the door to let Jeremy through.

"You weren't totally bored, were you?" she asked, closing the door behind her.

"No way," Jeremy said. "Believe me, *bored* isn't the word."

"Wow!" Tia said as the maitre d' led them through the elegant restaurant to their corner table. "I think I've seen this place on TV!"

"You did. It was on *Entertainment Tonight* last week. They interviewed one of those dorks from the WB here," Angel said with a grin.

"Hey! They're not dorks," Tia said, pretending to be offended. "They're just bad actors." She looked around in obvious awe, taking it all in. It was a vast space, broken into several different levels so that the diners at each table had a view of everyone else. They passed a table with an open bottle of Dom Pérignon sitting in an ice bucket between a stunning blonde and a distinguished older man.

Suddenly Tia clutched Angel's arm. "Oh my God. I think I see a Baldwin," she whispered.

Angel laughed. "Happy anniversary," he said, proudly escorting her to their table. She was wearing a blazing red dress, and her gorgeous brown eyes were wide with happiness. She looked absolutely radiant; even in this swank atmosphere he noticed she was drawing some admiring glances.

He pulled out her chair for her, and she sat down. "This is totally amazing," she said, fingering the ornate silverware.

"Well, I wanted something really special," Angel replied.

A waiter appeared and handed them menus. When Tia opened hers, her face fell. "Angel," she whispered. "This place is *really* expensive."

Angel fought to keep a straight face when he saw the prices. "Don't worry about it," he said as his stomach was invaded by butterflies. He'd known it would be expensive, but he had no idea anyone ever charged this much for food.

"I really don't think we should do this," Tia whispered, leaning forward. She glanced at the menu. "One appetizer here costs as much as a dinner for two at Emilio's. And the entrées cost as much as my dress!"

Angel felt beads of sweat appearing on his brow and told himself to chill. He had all that money from the track. He was covered. "It's a special occasion," he said, putting his hand over Tia's. "Besides, this is my present to you."

"But where are you going to get the money for this?" Tia looked around her warily, as if she was afraid someone was going to figure out they were posers and drop-kick them out the back door.

"I told you. Don't worry about it," he said, looking into her eyes. "Really, Tee. Let's just have a good time."

Tia bit her lip and took a deep breath. "Okay. But if they make us wash dishes afterward, you owe me a new dress. I don't think this one could take it."

A waiter appeared beside Tia and asked for her order. She studied the menu and finally said, "I think I'll just have the Caesar salad," and snapped her menu closed.

"Very good," the waiter replied, looking at Angel and waiting expectantly. Angel felt his face heat up. She didn't have to skimp. It was embarrassing.

"Look. They have grilled swordfish," he prompted. "Why don't you try that? You must be starving after cheerleading practice."

"Angel," Tia said quietly. "I *like* Caesar salad."

"Yeah, but that's what you always have." Angel silently willed her to just go along with him. The hovering waiter was making him tense. "Tonight's special."

Tia's stomach grumbled, and she laughed nervously. "All right," she said finally. "I'll try the swordfish. No salad, though. Just the fish."

"I'll have the filet mignon, medium rare," Angel said. "And let's start with some caviar."

Tia gaped at him as the waiter left. "Caviar? Isn't that like the most expensive thing on the menu?"

"We're celebrating." Angel held up his crystal water glass. "To three years with the most beautiful girl in California."

"The world," Tia corrected him automatically. Angel laughed as she held up her glass and shook her head. "This will be a night to remember, all right," she said.

The waiter returned with a silver tray, which he set in the middle of their table. On it were two tiny crystal bowls, each with its own miniature mother-of-pearl spoon. One bowl contained a mound of tiny gray eggs; the other, crème fraiche. Between them was a silver bowl full of triangular pieces of toasted brioche. Tia looked at the caviar hesitantly. "What do you think you're supposed to do with it?" she said.

Angel spooned a serving of caviar onto a piece of brioche, then added a little of the thick cream. "How's that look?" he said, handing it to Tia.

"I don't know. Here goes," she said, giggling nervously. She popped it into her mouth and chewed.

"Well?" Angel asked.

"It's delicious! It doesn't taste fishy at all." She held the rest of the piece out to Angel. He leaned forward and let her put it in his mouth.

"Wow!" he said as the taste exploded, filling his senses. "That is really good."

"It better be, considering how much—" Tia stopped in midsentence. "Sorry. Forget I said that." They continued eating in silence.

Angel did a quick calculation in his head. Each bite was costing him about seven dollars. He chewed and swallowed. *There goes an hour of cleaning tables at the Riot,* he thought. He managed to keep smiling and talking lightly with Tia, but the guilt was starting to take on a life of its own. What was he thinking, bringing her here? Why didn't he just let her have her salad? Did he really have to prove himself to some random waiter?

By the time they had finished the caviar, he was hardly tasting it at all.

"That was delicious," Maria said, pushing away her plate. "I can't believe I ate an entire seafood platter."

Ken dipped a fried shrimp into its tangy, spicy sauce and popped it in his mouth. "I know," he said. "It's so good, you can't stop." They were sitting outdoors on a weather-beaten deck, watching the sun slipping toward the ocean. The calls of distant seagulls drifted toward them over the sandy beach. The air was cool, and the other diners had chosen to eat inside, so they had the deck to themselves.

"I'm so glad you took me here, Ken," Maria said. "Even if I do weigh five pounds more now than I did this morning. It's so peaceful." Her face glowed in the flickering light of the candle burning in the glass cup between them. She looked beautiful.

"I love it out here with the smell of the ocean," Ken said.

Maria closed her eyes and inhaled. Ken could see her shoulders relax, and she took a few more breaths, a faint smile playing over her lips. She opened her eyes and saw Ken watching her, and her smile grew.

"Do you . . . want to go for a walk on the beach?" Ken said. "You weren't planning on dessert, were you?"

Maria laughed. "I can barely walk as it is. Let's go—it's almost time for the sunset."

Ken tucked the check and some money under the candle so it wouldn't blow away, and they made their way down the rickety stairs that led from the porch directly to the beach. They walked together quietly, watching the clouds on the horizon glow the color of peaches against the blue sky. The crash of the waves blurred together into a sleepy drone that Ken found extremely relaxing.

"Look," Maria said. The sun was resting right on the surface of the ocean. As they watched, it seemed to sink into the water until it looked like a fiery orange dome standing on the edge of the sea. "I can't remember the last time I watched the sunset," Maria said. "It's so beautiful."

They walked on in silence until they reached a mass of tangled seaweed, then stopped and listened to the waves. "This is the most relaxed I've been in a long time," Maria said. "School seems so far away right now, doesn't it?"

Ken scratched his head. "School? What's that? Wait, don't tell me," he said. "It's coming back. . . ."

Maria put her hands on her hips and waited.

"Nope," he concluded. "I guess it wasn't that important."

Maria tried to shove him playfully, but he dodged and darted away down the beach.

"Just try it," he yelled back.

"Oh, you're on!" Maria shouted back. She raced along the shore after him, tracing the edge of the water as the languid waves meandered in and out. Finally Ken felt her closing in on him and slowed down. At the last second he cupped his hands in the surf and flung a handful of water at her. It splashed over her bare legs and onto the bottom of her green cargo shorts.

Maria just stood there for a second, staring down at the wet spots. Then she looked up at him with an evil grin. "You are so done," she said. She ran to the water's edge, ignoring the waves sloshing over her sandals, and started splashing salty water at him with both hands.

Ken stood stock-still, his arms outstretched, and let the water rain down on him, leaving dark splotches on his khaki pants and maroon T-shirt. "You got me!" he said, sinking to his knees in the sand.

Maria raised her arms in triumph, but Ken darted forward and swept his whole arm across the foamy surf, sending a wave of seawater flying at her. She yelped and jumped backward, but her sandal caught in the sand, and she fell on her back.

"Time to beg for mercy!" Ken said. He scooped up a piece of seaweed and dangled it over her head.

Maria screamed and rolled away from him. "Eew! Get away from me!" she squealed. "Time-out!"

Ken laughed and tossed the smelly strand of kelp into the sea. He reached his hand down to Maria, and she let him pull her to her feet. Behind him the surf crashed.

Maria stood looking up at him, her eyes wide, her face open and cheerful. She really did look beautiful in the twilight. He took a step closer, every inch of him aching to just take her in his arms. He hadn't felt this way since . . .

Suddenly the thought of Olivia brought a wave of grief and guilt crashing down on him. For a second he had felt really happy. But as the realization over what he had almost done washed over him, his spirits crashed back to earth.

He couldn't get close to Maria. He couldn't do that to himself again.

"Maybe we should head back," he said gruffly. "It's getting late."

Ken Matthews

Dear Olivia,

It still hurts. I can't believe it, but it does.

It hurts less, though. Does that bother you? What am I saying? Of course it doesn't bother you. I know you wouldn't want me to hurt.

Tonight I went to the beach with Maria. It was the first time since the earthquake that I went out with another girl. And I was actually enjoying it . . . until I sort of freaked out.

When I got home, I went up to my room and lay on my bed in the dark. I must have just lain there for a few hours, thinking about you and thinking about her and feeling confused. I don't even know how I feel about her. I know it's nothing like what you and I had, but I don't know what it could become. . . .

I'm confusing myself again.

I must have fallen asleep because when

I woke up a little while later, I could feel you with me more than I have in a long time. And then I realized I can hang out with Maria and still keep you with me. You'll always be with me.

I think this is going to be my last letter. At least for a while. I know you understand.

I love you.

Love, Ken

CHAPTER
A Night to Forget?

7

"Thank you, Angel! I'll never forget this night," Tia said as they walked up to her front door.

She stopped and wrapped her arms around Angel's neck, gazing up into his eyes. He slipped his arms around her tiny waist, and he could hear her dress rustling when she nestled against him as he closed his eyes and pulled her closer. They kissed for a long time until they had to come up for air.

Angel held her against him, breathing in the comforting smell of freshly cut grass. Crickets chirped softly from somewhere in the yard, but otherwise the night was quiet, and the sky was perfectly clear. Angel could even see a few stars.

"I better go in," Tia said at last. "I'll see you tomorrow, okay?" She reached for the door.

"Tia?" he said. "I just want you to know, the last three years have been the best of my life. I love you."

"I love you too, Angel." She stood on her tiptoes and delicately touched her lips to his in a long, intimate kiss. Angel marveled at the way she could make his heart race after all this time. Tia disappeared inside, and Angel strolled back down the pathway to his car, grinning all the way.

But as he drove off, the romantic glow slowly faded. He stuck his hand in his pocket and felt his wallet. It was noticeably thinner.

Angel's heart squeezed with guilt. He'd spent the entire summer renting videos instead of going to movies, cooking dinner at home instead of taking Tia out, ordering water at the Riot instead of soda. For what? It would take him a month to earn back the money he'd spent tonight.

Suddenly a gnawing feeling permeated his stomach, as if a little mouse were chewing its way out. Why hadn't he just put the cash in the bank? He imagined the anniversary they could have had if he had listened to Tia. No stress, no guilt, just the two of them spending a quiet evening together. They could have relaxed and had a good time instead of hearing an imaginary cash register every time they lifted a fork.

He pulled into his driveway and sat there for a few minutes, staring blankly at the garage door. If his dad knew what he had just done, he would kill him. Or worse. Angel clenched his eyes shut, imagining his father's voice hammering into his head about what an irresponsible fool he was.

That was one conversation he definitely wanted to skip. He got out of the car and closed the door as softly as he could. The light was on in the living room. They couldn't still be up watching TV, could they? Angel tiptoed over to the window and peeked in. Both his parents' usual chairs were empty.

Angel opened the front door and walked softly toward the stairs. Keeping a watchful eye on the living room, he started tiptoeing up to his room . . . and ran smack into his father.

"Angel!" His father gave him a broad grin. "How'd it go tonight, son?"

"Fine," Angel said. Why was his dad smiling?

His father put a massive hand on his shoulder. "So, where did you two go?"

Angel shrugged. "Oh . . . I don't know. Some restaurant. I don't remember the name."

His father laughed. His powerful shoulders bulged as he stuck his hands into the pockets of his black jeans. Despite the liberal sprinkling of gray in his close-cropped, salt-and-pepper hair, at six-feet-two and two hundred twenty pounds he was still an imposing figure. "I'm the same way," he said, relaxing against the wall. "Your mother can remember every one of our dates, but to me they just run together. I guess women are just better at that stuff. I'm sure I'll get every detail from Tia next time I see her." He chuckled again.

Okay, so you won't ever be seeing Tia again, Dad.

Angel tried to laugh, but he couldn't seem to get enough air.

"You said it was your anniversary, right? Did you take her somewhere nice?" his father asked.

"Uh, pretty nice. I mean, it was okay," Angel said.

His father cleared his throat. "You know, I think I was a little rough on you before. You've been working hard, and you deserved a night out." He stared down at his worn plaid slippers. "I know we don't always see eye to eye, but your mother and I think you're maturing into a fine young man." He raised his eyes and stared at Angel, as if sizing him up. "Not as fast as we would like sometimes, but I don't want you to think we're not proud of you. It means a lot to us that we can trust you to behave responsibly."

"Thanks," Angel said, wishing he could crawl under a rock.

His father clapped him on the back, and Angel had to grab the banister to steady himself. "Well, better get to bed now. I expect you to be up at six o'clock tomorrow, ready to go to work. You had your fun, but the celebration's over."

"Don't worry," Angel said, swallowing hard. "I know."

Jessica clutched her books to her chest and held her breath. There was no way around it. She was going to have to walk right past them.

A bunch of El Carro football players were standing together in a group, laughing. If she hurried, she could get by before they noticed her.

Fixing her gaze rigidly on the doorway at the end of the hall, Jessica quickened her pace. She saw one of the guys watch her as she sped by, but no one said anything. Maybe Elizabeth was right. Maybe Melissa's suicide attempt really had replaced her as the school's main gossip topic.

"Yo, Wakefield!"

Her heart stopped. Then again, maybe not.

"Hey, Wakefield, a few of us are looking for a date Friday night. What do you say?"

She ducked her head and upped the pace, her eyes stinging.

"*Hey!*"

The yell sliced through the background noise in the hall, and Jessica froze. Everyone stopped talking. For a second she didn't dare to look up. But when she did, she was amazed to see that no one was looking at her; they were all gaping at something behind her.

Jessica spun and saw a large, crew-cut, El Carro jock pinned against the wall. He was gasping for breath. Someone had grabbed the front of his jacket and wasn't letting go. She couldn't see who it was until a few freshmen shifted to the right and gave her a clear view.

101

The familiar blond hair and muscular build took a moment to register. *Will?*

"What are you doing, man? Let me go!" the jock snapped.

"Not until you shut the hell up," Will said through clenched teeth.

"Fine. Whatever," the guy said.

Will shoved him one last time, slamming him against the cinder-block wall, and then pulled away.

"What's wrong with you?" the jock demanded, straightening his sweater.

Will looked around at the tiny crowd that had gathered, and his face went from flushed to four-alarm fire. Jessica held her breath as he shook his head and started to walk away.

Good, she thought. Will needed to cool off, or there was going to be a serious fight here. The tension was thicker than LA smog.

Then she looked up and caught the crew-cut jock's eye. A slow smile spread across his face. "I get it. So, Will's got a soft spot for the school slut," he said. "What did she do for you that made you so friendly?"

Silence.

Will turned and stepped up to the jock. Their faces were just inches apart. "I told you to shut up, Beckford," he said quietly. "Don't push me." His arms were at his sides, but Jessica could see that his hands were clenched into fists.

For a few tense moments the bigger guy looked like he was about to say something. He glanced at his buddies on either side and then met Will's gaze. "Dude, why are you suddenly defending her?" He sounded disgusted.

Jessica saw Will go rigid, and for a moment she thought the Beckford guy was dead. But then Will took a deep, audible breath through his nose and backed off.

"I'm defending her," he said, turning his head to look Jessica in the eye, "because nothing ever happened. She never did any of the things we said she did."

A gray haze swept over Jessica's line of vision, and she was sure she was about to black out. She reached out and touched the cool, mayonnaise-colored wall, and the feel of the grain beneath her fingers grounded her. She leaned against it for support as the people around her started buzzing with questions.

"*What?*" Beckford spat, his face scrunched up in confusion. "What are you talking about?"

Will looked around at the group and put his hands on his hips. "I should have said something a long time ago." He paused and shook his head, looking at the floor. "But I'm saying it now. None of that stuff ever happened. Those rumors are going to stop, right now." He looked at each of his friends in turn. "Does anybody have a problem with that?"

Finally Beckford held up his hands. "Naw, man," he said, backing away. "Whatever."

As the jocks started to move off, a few of them threw curious glances in Jessica's direction. She blushed but refused to look away. Then the rest of the crowd dispersed. Although Jessica got several more confused stares, no one said anything as they walked by.

The bell rang, but Jessica couldn't move. Hot tears formed in her eyes. Will had finally told the truth. He'd finally, *finally* told the truth.

Jeremy closed his eyes and inhaled the soothing aroma of roasted coffee emanating from the cappuccino machine. It had been totally crazed tonight at House of Java, and he was glad. The more he had to concentrate on work, the less time there was to worry about Jessica.

He filled the coffee filter, tamped it down, and twisted it into locked position. With his other hand he stuck the metal pitcher of milk into position. Then he twisted the knob, sending hot steam surging into the milk. The steamed milk foamed and gurgled as he raised and lowered the pitcher. At the exact moment the espresso machine dribbled to a stop, he grabbed a tall glass, poured in the coffee and some chocolate syrup, and topped it off with steamed milk. He spooned some foam onto the top, dusted it with cocoa, and slid it across the counter. The whole operation had taken barely thirty seconds. "Double mocha," he said. "Who's next?"

A slim girl with long, chestnut hair was standing across the counter, staring at him. She was wearing a pale blue sundress that matched her eyes. "Jeremy?" she asked. He squinted at her. There was something familiar about her face, but he couldn't place it. "We need to talk."

He glanced down the counter. There was no one waiting. But something about the girl made him uneasy. "I'm sorry," he said. "Do I know you?"

"It's about Jessica."

Suddenly Jeremy remembered where he had seen her. She had been with those girls who had insulted Jessica at Trent's party. He recognized her pale skin and those huge, ice blue eyes. He remembered thinking at the time that she looked like a porcelain doll. Melissa, her name was. It was the same girl, he was sure of it.

"If I want to know something about Jessica, I'll ask her myself," he said flatly.

She didn't even blink. "What would you say if I told you she was seeing someone behind your back?" she asked.

Jeremy felt a wave of panic. *The gifts!* Did she know something about them? His right hand was gripping the sugar jar so hard, he was afraid it would break, but he kept his voice calm. "I told you, I'm not interested in anything you have to say," he repeated. "Do you really think I'd believe you over her? Why do you care what Jessica does anyway?"

Melissa crossed her arms and stared back at him passively. "Because she fooled around with my boyfriend behind my back. I just thought I'd warn you before she betrayed you too."

Jeremy's heart was in his throat. "You're lying."

She shrugged and rested her hand on her trendy leather purse. "Fine. It's not my problem," she said. "I just thought you deserved to know the truth. If you don't believe me, ask Jessica why she has a date with Will Simmons on Friday." She raised one eyebrow, leveled him with a stare, and then turned and calmly walked out of the shop. Jeremy stared after her, stunned.

"Excuse me? Hello? Can I get a decaf cappuccino?" A guy in a rugby shirt was rapping on the counter.

"I'm on break," Jeremy said. He took off his apron and walked to the bathroom, touching his coworker's shoulder as he left so she would know she was on her own. He locked the door and stood staring at himself in the mirror, trying to keep from shaking.

Were the gifts he had found in Jessica's room from Will Simmons? Could she really be cheating on him? No. He couldn't let Melissa get to him.

There had to be some other explanation. Maybe they really *were* from an ex-boyfriend.

He splashed water onto his face and peered at his bloodshot eyes in the mirror. Who was he kidding? Either the gifts or the warning alone he could ignore. But what were the odds that they were both just a coincidence?

He wasn't looking forward to this, but it looked like he had no choice. He and Jessica were going to have to have a little talk.

melissa fox

I am going to get Will back. It's that simple. I'm not boasting when I say this, but I always get what I want in the end. And I'll tell you why.

The secret to getting what you want is to stay focused on your goal. It's like dieting. Most people quit after a week. If you want to succeed, you've got to have a plan and stick to it, no matter what.

The same thing is true with controlling guys. Sure, I'm suffering a temporary setback with Will right now. But the difference between me and most other people is, I know what I did wrong. I let Jessica get to me.

The big picture is Will. Jessica only matters because she affects Will. The real battle is being fought in Will's head, and this gives me a big advantage because I know how Will thinks.

So, no more emotional outbursts, no personal vendettas. I know how to get Will back. And if Jessica Wakefield happens to get hurt along the way, that will be purely a coincidence.

CHAPTER
No More Secrets
8

"What a beautiful day," Jessica said. "Have you ever seen weather so perfect?"

There was no cheerleading practice today, so she was standing in the sunny SVH courtyard with Elizabeth and Maria before their *Oracle* meeting, watching the water in the fountain soar and splash into the carved stone pool. She had never noticed how relaxing the sound of the fountain was before. It was like being at the beach.

Maria laughed.

"What?" Jessica asked.

"It's just funny you said that. The weather has been like this almost every day for about three weeks."

"Well, I guess I'm just noticing it now," Jessica said.

A breeze lifted a few strands of Jessica's hair and made them flutter across her face, but she didn't move. Their feathery touch felt good against her cheek. In fact, everything seemed to feel better now.

"It's not surprising, really. You've had a lot on your mind," Elizabeth said.

" 'A lot' is an understatement," Maria said. "But I bet things will get better now, after Will's little hero act."

"I told you he might not be such a bad guy," Elizabeth said. "You can't jump to conclusions about people."

"Maybe you're right," Jessica said. She raised her arms to the sunny sky and stretched luxuriantly. "I'm just glad he finally told the truth. It's like I have closure now and I never have to think about Will Simmons again."

Oh, yeah? Then how come you haven't thought of anything else all day? she thought.

It was pretty amazing how Will had taken on the whole group like that, completely outnumbered, and they had all backed down. Maybe it was all those years playing quarterback. There was something about him that made people listen. Something captivating, something that made you want to . . .

"We've got to get to the meeting," Maria said, glancing at her watch.

Elizabeth sighed. "Okay." She looked at Jessica, her eyes tired. "I'll see you at home later, okay?"

"Definitely," Jessica responded. "I didn't plan anything tonight, so we can just hang out and talk."

Elizabeth gave her a hug. "Thanks, Jess," she whispered. Maria waved good-bye, and the two of them hurried off.

Jessica closed her eyes, feeling the afternoon sun on her face. It was too nice a day to spend inside. Maybe she should go watch football practice. It would be nice to see Will in action. . . .

She stopped herself. What was she thinking? She had a boyfriend. A *perfect* boyfriend, ten times better than Will. If she was going to visit someone, it would be Jeremy. She got in her car and headed for House of Java. Big Mesa didn't have football practice today—the coaches were at a meeting or something—so naturally Jeremy had booked a double shift. Seeing him would push these thoughts of Will out of her head for sure.

She tuned in to her favorite radio station and drove with the windows open, singing loudly. By the time she pulled into the small parking lot next to the coffeehouse, she couldn't wait to see Jeremy. She burst through the door, ran to the counter, grabbed Jeremy around the waist, and gave him a big kiss.

Jeremy looked startled. He obviously hadn't expected to see her.

"Jessica!" Ally stuck her head out of her office as if Jessica's arrival had triggered her radar. "I'm glad to see you. Suzanne called in sick, and I'm short tonight. Can you come in later, around six?"

"Sorry, I can't," Jessica said, moving away from Jeremy. Her manager hated public displays of affection. "I promised my sister—"

"I really need you here," Ally said. Several strands of her brown hair were hanging loose from her ponytail, and she looked exhausted.

Jessica felt Jeremy's warm breath on her neck. "You know, I'm working tonight," he whispered in her ear. "Why don't you come in too? Can't you see Liz when you get home?"

Jessica grinned as his closeness sent shivers down her neck and arm. "All right," she called to Ally. "I'll be here." Jeremy gave her a quick kiss on the cheek and took off his apron.

"I'm taking my break now, Ally," he said.

"You just had a break, Aames," Ally pointed out.

"Okay. So I won't take any more for the rest of the night," Jeremy said.

Ally shrugged. "Suit yourself."

Jeremy turned to Jessica. "Want a cup of coffee, Jess?" he asked, already working on a mochaccino.

"Thanks," Jessica said as he handed her the steaming cup.

She carried it to a table in the corner, then sank into an upholstered armchair. "I'm so glad this isn't one of those glass-and-Formica places with the tiny round tables about five feet high," she said. "It's like sitting around a flagpole. And those stools get uncomfortable after about three minutes." She stretched out her legs. "Give me an armchair any day."

Jeremy sat on the edge of the seat opposite her. "Yeah," he said shortly.

Jessica's brow furrowed, and she set her coffee on the table. "Is something wrong?" she asked.

He was rolling and unrolling the bottom of his blue T-shirt between his fingers. "Listen, there's something I wanted to talk to you about."

"Sure. What is it?" Jessica asked. She hoped something hadn't happened with his father. The last thing Jeremy needed was more trauma in his life.

"When I was in your room the other day, I found . . . something." His eye was twitching, and he only looked up at her for a second before focusing on his busy hands.

Jessica's heart skipped a beat. This didn't sound good. "Yeah?" she prodded.

Jeremy squeezed his eyes shut, and the worry lines on his forehead deepened. "I . . . I wasn't snooping." He was struggling to get out the words. "It was in a shopping bag . . . and you told me to clean out under your bed."

Suddenly Jessica sat bolt upright, knocking the table with her knee and almost spilling her coffee. The gifts from Will! How could she have been so stupid?

"You found the . . . presents?" she asked, her mind reeling for an explanation.

Jeremy was eyeing her closely. "So they were gifts," he said.

Just act casual, she told herself. *Don't let him think this is a big deal.*

"Yeah . . . well, kind of," she said breezily. "They were actually from a secret admirer. Can you believe it?"

She could still play it off as a funny story—as long as he didn't ask who it was. It had been totally awkward when Will and Jeremy ran into each other at the ice cream shop. They had stared each other down like wrestlers before a match. Jessica could almost smell the testosterone.

Jeremy exhaled slowly. "A secret admirer? When?" he asked.

She took a deep breath. There was no point in lying about this. He would know, and at this point she wanted to come clean. As clean as possible anyway. "Last week," she said, trying not to look guilty.

"Last week!" Jeremy blurted out. "Why didn't you tell me?"

"I . . . I really didn't think it was such a big deal," Jessica answered truthfully. "I mean, I blew the guy off, so what was the point in freaking you out over nothing?"

Jeremy rubbed his temples. "Well, I wish you had told me. I mean, how would you feel, finding love letters under your boyfriend's bed?"

"I'm sorry! But you were dealing with so much other stuff already, I didn't want to stress you out for no reason." Jessica twisted her fingers together in her lap.

"Yeah, but now I'm stressed out because you *didn't* tell me," Jeremy said.

"I know." Jessica nodded. "No more secrets, I promise."

"So . . . who was it?" Jeremy asked quietly. New wrinkles appeared on his forehead, as if he were preparing to be slapped.

Jessica's stomach clenched and unclenched. *Don't make me do this,* she thought, her eyes pleading. But he just sat there unmoving, like a prisoner waiting to hear his sentence.

Jessica hesitated, biting her lip. "Will Simmons," she said finally.

Jeremy actually winced. "Is there anything else you wanted to tell me?" he asked, his eyes hard.

"What do you mean?" Jessica asked.

"Like, do you have a date with him?"

Suddenly Jessica felt like the room was one of those amusement-park rides that spins faster and faster until the floor drops out. Where would Jeremy get the idea that she was cheating on him? She'd told him she blew Will off. "Of course not!" she said, gripping her chair. "How could you even ask me that? I told him I had a boyfriend!"

She could see Jeremy's jaw muscles working

under his skin. "That's not what I heard," he said. "I heard you and Will have a date this Friday."

The spinning room suddenly lurched to a halt. "And you *believed* it?" Jessica said furiously. The people at the next table glanced over at her, but she ignored them. "Who told you that anyway?"

"It doesn't matter," Jeremy answered. "But it's kind of a coincidence, don't you think?" There was an edge to his voice, and his fingers were digging into the frayed armrests of his own chair. "And since you didn't tell me about those gifts, yeah, it made me wonder a little. That's why I wanted to talk to you. Just to get it all straightened out." He stared at her, his normally gentle eyes looking cold and impenetrable.

"I'm sorry I didn't tell you about those stupid gifts, okay? But I didn't ask for them! What was I supposed to do? If I *had* told you, you would only have gotten upset!" Jessica felt her lips trembling, and tears started forming in her eyes. She took another deep breath to hold them back and stared at him. "I can't believe this. How could you listen to some stupid rumor? Don't you trust me?"

Jeremy squeezed his head in his hands. "I didn't say I believed it. Look, I'm sorry I even brought it up. Let's just forget it, okay?"

Jessica wiped her eyes. "I know I'm overreacting—I just thought I was finally done with people

118

lying about me behind my back. I seriously can't take this anymore."

"Jess . . . I'm . . . I'm really sorry," he said, his voice softening. "You're right. I've just been totally stressed out."

"I've got to get out of here." Jessica stood up. She felt suffocated. She knew she hadn't been completely honest with Jeremy, but she couldn't handle the fact that the rumor mill had finally gotten to him. Just when she thought it was over.

Jeremy stood and hugged her, but Jessica was rigid. All she could bring herself to do was pat him quickly on the back.

"When you come in later, we'll just start over, okay?" Jeremy asked.

"Yeah. Sure," Jessica said. She pulled away from him and walked out the door without looking back. *Start over,* she thought. Too bad she couldn't just start her whole life over.

"This sucks," Ken said, running his hands through his hair. "I am so sick of studying."

You've only been doing it for a couple of days, Maria thought, trying hard not to laugh. "Shhh," she said. "We're in a library, remember?"

Ken slumped to the table facedown and covered his head with his hands. "I'm serious. I really don't think I can do this anymore."

"Yes, you can. You just have to keep at it, that's

all." Maria shook him by the shoulder. Even without working out, he still felt as solid as a rock. "Come on, you wouldn't expect to be good at football if you didn't practice every day, would you? What would your coach tell you right now?"

Ken sat up straight and stiffened his back. "'Give it everything you've got, every single second, or I don't want you on my team,'" he said in a deep voice. "'Football requires a total commitment.'" Then he slumped back down again.

"There you go," Maria said. "Study that way, and you'll get A's."

He crumpled the piece of paper in front of him into a ball. "I just don't know how much longer I can sit still like this! I feel like hitting somebody."

Maria couldn't help staring at his hands, callused from his weekend landscaping job, as he wadded the defenseless paper into an ever smaller ball. "What's wrong? Mr. Tough Guy Football Player can't take it?" she teased, trying to distract herself from thinking about their just-this-side-of-romantic dinner the night before. This was Ken. Emotionally closed-off, in-perpetual-mourning Ken. "Is this nerd stuff too hard for you?"

He groaned, and a girl at the next table glared at them. "If I look at this book one more time, I'm going to rip it in half," he whispered, hoisting his hefty history text with one hand.

"Give me that!" Maria snatched the book with a

grin. "Come to think of it, I bet that's why they invented football. To keep the jocks and all their pent-up hormones from tearing apart the library."

"You're probably right. Guys would go crazy without sports." Ken laughed shortly, the realization of what he was saying obviously setting in. "I guess that explains a lot, doesn't it?" He stared down at the table, fidgeting with the corner of his notebook.

"You mean *you're* going crazy?" Maria said cautiously. "Because you quit the team?" Ken didn't answer, and Maria wasn't sure if she should push it. She had made the mistake of asking him once if he missed football, and he had almost bitten her head off. She'd been avoiding the subject ever since, and it was obviously still a sore spot. Still, they had been spending a lot more time together. Maybe now she could talk about it without risking bodily harm.

Ken rested his head in his hands. "I guess I better learn to study. That's all I've got left." He shifted in his seat. "I used to be able to count on getting into any college I wanted on a football scholarship. Last year every school in the country was recruiting me. But that's all gone now. With my grades I'll be lucky to get into community college."

He stared out the window, and Maria knew he was thinking about the practice going on outside at that very moment.

"You really miss football, don't you?" she said quietly. He didn't answer, and she waited silently for several seconds. Finally he shrugged, but his slumped posture spoke volumes.

"Why don't you just join the team again?" Maria asked.

Ken grimaced. "It's not that simple. The coach would never let me. I told you what he's like. It's all or nothing with him. He hates quitters, and I quit."

"It's worth a shot, though, isn't it? If you explained what happened, I'm sure he'd understand." She paused and cleared her throat. "What if you told him the reason you didn't want to play before was you weren't sure you could give the team one hundred percent and you wouldn't accept anything less from yourself? Coaches love that stuff."

Ken snorted. "Give him a taste of his own medicine, you mean? I'd like to see what he'd say to that." His face fell. "Seriously, though, he made it pretty clear that I had to decide one way or the other and then live with it."

"So what? I still think you should talk to him. What have you got to lose?"

He didn't answer, but she could tell he was weakening. His blue eyes were thoughtful, and he was lightly tapping his fist against his mouth, which he always did when he was concentrating. Maria leaned back in her chair and stifled a small smile.

She hadn't realized how much she'd learned about Ken in the past few weeks.

Finally he sighed and leaned forward to slide his history book away from her. He cracked it open in front of him and stared at the page. All the while Maria watched him discreetly through her lashes. "You're right," he said coolly, as if the thought didn't excite him at all. "What have I got to lose?"

Jessica ran up the long staircase to her room at the Fowlers'. Just two more weeks and she'd be free of this place. Maybe then she would feel like she had a fresh start.

What she really wanted was to collapse in her own bed, in her own room, with the door locked and the phone unplugged. Definitely with the phone unplugged. But even so, Will would probably still find some way to worm his way into her life. Why did he always have to ruin everything? Jeremy had been the one light in her otherwise bleak life, and now Will had even managed to mess that up.

She rummaged through a pile of clothes on the floor, looking for something she wouldn't mind spilling coffee on. She had learned the hard way not to wear anything she really liked to work. She found some old black jeans and a black T-shirt and pulled them on. It was going to be a long, miserable night of awkwardness with Jeremy. She might as well dress for it.

There was a quick knock on the door, and then Elizabeth walked in. "Hey," she said, sitting down on the edge of Jessica's bed.

"Hey," Jessica answered, tucking in her shirt.

Elizabeth stretched out on Jessica's bed and stared at the ceiling. "God, what a week. I'm so glad we have a whole evening just to hang out."

Uh-oh. Jessica's heart sank. "Liz, you're going to kill me, but I have to go to work."

Elizabeth sat up abruptly. "I thought you were free tonight."

"I know, but Ally begged—"

"Jess!" Elizabeth blurted out. "This is the third time you've blown me off this week!"

Jessica sank onto the bed next to her, a feeling of wretchedness descending on her like a cloud of toxic smoke. She seemed to be having this effect on almost everyone lately. "I'm really, really sorry," she said. "Believe me, I would so much rather stay here with you. Jeremy and I just had this big fight, and I don't know how I'm going to—"

Elizabeth jumped up and faced Jessica. "God, I feel *so* sorry for you, Jess," she said. "It must be *so* hard having the captains of two different football teams fighting over you all the time. How could I have *possibly* been upset just because Conner never wants to speak to me again."

124

Elizabeth spun on her heel and headed for the door. Jessica was so stunned, she could barely make her lips move. "Liz—"

"No," Elizabeth said, pausing with her hand on the doorknob. "Thanks for helping me put it all in perspective. You'd better get to work now. That is, unless you come up with something better to do in the next five minutes." With that, she stalked out, slamming the door behind her.

Jessica stared at the door, unable to move. Elizabeth never, *ever* lost it like that. Jessica knew her sister was hurting, but she'd thought it was just a standard broken heart that would take some time to get over. But that tirade was another thing entirely.

She got up and headed for the door. Elizabeth was right. She'd been a selfish brat. Ally would just have to deal with being short staffed for a little while. But when Jessica opened the door, she came face-to-face with Lila.

"Hi, Jess." Lila stood with her arms crossed casually.

"Lila," Jessica said, pulling up short.

"How are you?" Lila asked. Somehow she had managed to ooze by Jessica into the room and was examining her eyelashes in the mirror.

"How am I?" Jessica said, eyeing her suspiciously. "Why? What makes you so chatty today?"

Lila pursed her lips. "I just wanted to see how

you were holding up after that big scene with Will in the hall."

Jessica frowned. "Sniffing around for gossip! Of course! That's why you're suddenly speaking to me again."

Lila picked up Jessica's newest lipstick and rolled it out an inch or so, then held it thoughtfully up to the light. "Gossip? No, I'm not looking for gossip. There was plenty of that today already, don't you think?" She dabbed the lipstick on her wrist and examined it.

"What do you mean?" Jessica asked. She knew it was exactly what Lila wanted her to say, but her curiosity got the better of her.

Lila shrugged and strolled over to the window. "Well, obviously everyone was impressed by Will's little display today. But I kept telling them that doesn't necessarily mean you two are together or anything. I'm sure there's another explanation. Right?" She turned and stared at Jessica, twisting her long, glossy hair around her finger. "I mean, I can't think of one offhand, but—"

"I don't have to explain myself to you or anyone else," Jessica said, snatching up her purse and keys. "I'm out of here."

Lila narrowed her eyes. "Wow. You don't have to be so defensive."

"There's nothing to be defensive about." Jessica glared at Lila. "Will finally told the truth, that's all."

"So you're not together," Lila said.

"No! We are not together!" Jessica spat. "God! Why can't everyone just leave me alone?"

Jessica walked out of her room and slammed the door behind her. She rushed down the stairs and through the wide foyer, trying to catch her breath. This was unbelievable. Even when Will did something good, it backfired on her. She could just imagine what Melissa was going to do if she believed the rumors that Jessica and Will were seeing each other.

As soon as she was safely outside, Jessica leaned against the door and closed her eyes, her mind reeling with images of Will, Melissa, Lila, Cherie, Gina. She couldn't go through this again.

Never again.

Jeremy Aames

<u>English</u> <u>Lit</u> <u>Homework</u> <u>Assignment</u>
Write a short essay about the play *Othello*.
What lessons can we learn from this play?

In William Shakespeare's play <u>Othello</u> the main character, Othello, is driven crazy with jealousy and kills his wife, Desdemona. Othello is sure she has been unfaithful to him, even though Desdemona is completely innocent.

Othello is convinced of his wife's guilt by his trusted yet evil adviser, Iago, who poisons his mind with lies. Instead of trusting his faithful wife Othello believes Iago, and by the time he finds out the truth, it is too late.

The message of this play is, don't jump to conclusions about the people you love. Someone could be lying to you for unknown, selfish reasons. If you're not careful, you'll go crazy with jealousy and ruin everything. Of course, in real life it's not always easy to tell who is lying and who is telling the truth. No matter how fair you try to be, you can still go crazy wondering who the liar is.

Jessica's pulse was just starting to return to normal when a Chevy Blazer turned into the circular driveway. A very familiar Chevy Blazer.

"Not now," Jessica whimpered to herself. But sure enough, Will Simmons climbed out of the car, wearing khaki pants and a pale blue oxford shirt and looking completely perfect.

Jessica pushed herself away from the front door. She had to get him out of here. What if Lila saw him? The nonfact that they were secretly seeing each other would be all over school by tomorrow morning. If Jeremy was jealous now, wait till that got back to him. And somehow Jessica knew it would.

"Will, I was just leaving," Jessica said, heading past him toward the Jeep. She caught a glimpse of Will's confused expression but kept going, fumbling with her keys.

"Jessica, wait," Will called, jogging to catch up with her.

Jessica tried to ignore her pounding heart, irritated by her own excitement. "I really have to go," she said. "I'm late for work." She glanced over her shoulder, wondering which of the twenty or so windows Lila might be peeking out of. Fortunately the house was so big that she was probably hundreds of feet from a window. But Lila's room did face the street . . .

"No problem," Will said. "I just wanted to ask you something."

If he asks me out on a date, I'm going to just die right here, Jessica thought. "What?" she asked, unlocking the car door.

Will looked away, and the shifting shadows cast by the tree above them seemed to caress his rugged features. He cleared his throat. "I . . . uh . . . I found out I'm supposed to organize this kidnap thing because I'm captain of the football team? Todd told me you did it last year, and he said maybe you would help." He looked at her, and his penetrating gray-blue eyes sent a shiver up her spine. This was definitely not helping.

"The kidnap?" Jessica asked dumbly. "You're kidding, right?"

"No . . . ," Will said slowly. "Look, I know I'm not your favorite person right now, but I really need your help with this thing. You're the only one who's dealt with it before and—"

"You know what? Fine," Jessica said. She checked over her shoulder again. "But can we talk about this later? I really have to go."

He shrugged. "Sure. I'm kind of busy the rest of this week, so is Friday night good for you? We could meet at First and Ten after practice. Around seven?"

Jessica mentally flipped through her date book. She was off work Friday night, and so far, she had no plans. "Okay. I'll see you then."

Will grinned. "Great."

Jessica opened her car door as Will started to walk away, and then it hit her.

Friday night with Will. That was exactly what Jeremy had said. She was making that stupid rumor come true! If anyone spotted her and Will alone in a restaurant, right after she'd sworn they didn't have a date that night, her relationship with Jeremy would be roadkill.

"Will! Hold on," she said. He turned as he opened his car door. The wind ruffled his hair, and their eyes locked. It took Jessica a moment to find her voice.

"It's just that . . . I was thinking . . . since Tia is the captain of the team now, don't you think she should come too?"

Will's face betrayed no emotion. "Yeah," he said, nodding. "Right."

"Cool. I'll tell her tomorrow at practice," Jessica said, relief surging through her. She had dodged a bullet on that one, no question. No one could say anything if Tia was there with them.

Will looked at the ground as if he was thinking

something through. "Well," he said finally. "I guess I better go."

"Will—" The word slipped out of her mouth before she knew what she was going to say. He stopped, and she clutched the door handle on the Jeep. "I wanted to thank you. For what you said today."

"Don't thank me," he said. "I should have said something a long time ago."

Their eyes met again, and although her heart was pounding, she couldn't tear her eyes away. It was as if everything that had happened in the last few weeks had suddenly dropped away and they were standing face-to-face, exactly as they had the night they first kissed. There were a hundred unspoken thoughts hanging in the air between them. She suddenly felt dizzy.

"Jessica—"

"I really have to go," she said. She slid into the Jeep, gunned the engine, and drove away without looking back.

Jeremy glanced at his watch. It was six-thirteen— just like the last time he had checked, ten seconds ago. Where was she?

Ally stuck her head out of her office, and her eyes swept the room. "Have you seen Jessica?" she said. She looked exhausted, and the gray of her sweatshirt seemed to be seeping into her skin and hair.

"No, but I know she had to go home and change.

And you know how bad traffic is at rush hour—"

The door swung open, and Jessica burst in, looking flushed. "Sorry I'm late, Ally," she said.

Ally let out a relieved sigh. "I'm just glad you could make it. The evening rush has been crazy since the bookstore down the block started staying open late. Why don't you guys refill everything before it gets too busy?"

"Okay," Jessica said as Ally disappeared back into her office.

"What happened?" Jeremy whispered. He wanted to hug her, but he kept his hands at his sides, wondering if she was still mad at him.

"Oh, nothing," Jessica said, looking away. "I just got held up." She tied her apron behind her, then grabbed a dishrag and started wiping down the counter, her back to him.

Jeremy felt an icy tightness in his gut, somewhere between anxiety and nausea. He cautiously put his hand on her shoulder. "I'm really sorry about before," he said.

"Forget about it," she said, giving him a quick, tense smile. "I'm sorry too."

He shook his head. "I mean, the idea of you seeing someone behind my back is . . . Well, I know you would never do something like that."

"Let's just drop it, okay? Please?" She kept scrubbing vigorously. Jeremy stood there a moment, wondering what to do. Things still didn't feel comfortable

135

between them, but he didn't want to push it. He tried to think of a safe, casual topic.

"So . . . what are you doing Friday?" he said.

She lowered her head and started scrubbing faster. "Not much," she said. "I'm meeting Tia and . . . some guys from the football team to plan the football kidnap."

"Turning to a life of crime?" Jeremy asked, smiling.

Jessica stopped working and turned to him with a thin smile. "It's an SVH tradition. One Saturday morning the cheerleaders and football players all get dragged out of bed and have to go out to breakfast in their pajamas. I have to help plan it."

"Sounds like fun," Jeremy said.

She sighed. "Yeah. It usually is." Her voice was distant, and Jeremy found himself acutely missing the easy banter they normally shared. He thought about apologizing again, but he had a feeling that would just make her more tense.

"So, do you want to make plans for Saturday?" Jeremy suggested. "Maybe we could go to the beach."

"I'd love to, but I have to help pick out furniture for our new house on Saturday," she said. "Besides, I really have to spend some time with Liz after canceling on her today." She bent down, opened one of the cabinets under the counter, and started pulling out supplies.

Jeremy stood watching her uncertainly, fighting

off panic. He felt like a child lost in a supermarket. Was she avoiding him, or was he just being paranoid? There was no way he could ask her. He'd definitely used up his allotment of accusations for the day.

"That's cool," he said evenly. "I hope you find some good stuff."

"Yeah," Jessica said, keeping her head tucked inside the cabinet. She hadn't met his eye once during the whole conversation.

"Excuse me? Can I get a cappuccino?"

Startled, Jeremy checked the counter and found a girl about his age there, digging through her pocketbook for her wallet.

"Sure," Jeremy said.

He went through the motions slowly, feeling light-headed. If Jessica was mad, he could deal with it. She wasn't the type to hold it in if she was angry, though. If she wasn't mad, then why was she avoiding him?

Angel was standing behind the bar at the Riot on Wednesday evening, enjoying a rare slow period, when Conner walked up and slumped onto a bar stool. He looked like he hadn't showered or shaved since the last time Angel had seen him.

"What's up?" Angel asked.

"What would I have to do to make you give me a real drink?" Conner asked.

"Bail me out of jail, pay my lawyer, and find me a new job," Angel said without missing a beat.

Conner cracked a quick smile. "I'll have a Coke."

Angel filled a tall glass with ice and soda and set it on the counter. Conner drained half the glass in one swallow.

"Whoa! Take it easy," Angel said. "I hope you're not driving home tonight, buddy."

"So, how was the track?" Conner asked, staring into his soda.

Angel leaned over and forced a casual grin. "You should have come with me, man. I could have used you to help carry home my winnings." No point in telling Conner he'd blown most of the cash already.

"That's how they all sound at first," Conner said. "Try asking one of those bums who crawl around under the bleachers looking for half-eaten hot dogs how he ended up there." He set down his damp glass and wiped his hands on his faded black T-shirt. Angel thought he recognized the stain on his jeans from Monday afternoon.

"Sour grapes, my man," Angel said. He scooped a couple of empties off the bar and tossed them in the recycling bin. He didn't remember seeing any down-and-out types at the track. Everybody had just seemed to be having a good time. Conner always had to put the darkest spin on things. "I'm telling you, you should have been there. I cleaned up. I may have to go back just to get rid of some of my extra winnings."

"Yeah, right." Conner took another gulp of soda.

But even as Conner shot down the idea, Angel started to really consider it. Maybe he should go again. Then he could win back the money he'd spent and put it in the bank.

Angel put a fresh stack of napkins on the bar and wiped his forehead against his sleeve. "Seriously, do you want to come with me next time?" he said. "It'll be more fun with company."

"Losing money is fun?" Conner asked.

"I wouldn't know. I haven't lost yet," he countered.

"The operative word being *yet*." Conner raised an eyebrow and drained his soda. His self-satisfied attitude was starting to bug Angel.

"All right, if you don't want to come, don't come," Angel said. "But I've got Friday afternoon off, so I'm going to swing by the track until Tia's done with practice. I'll just meet up with you guys later."

"Whatever," Conner said. He stood up, pulled a couple of dollars out of his pocket, and tossed them on the counter. Angel felt an irritated blush rise to his cheeks as Conner turned and sauntered away. Where did he get off, trying to tell Angel what to do? He was the person who had talked him into betting in the first place.

"Yeah, I'll meet up with you later," Angel muttered

to himself. "I'll be the one in the long, black limo." He smiled wryly and turned around to finish cleaning up the bar.

Ken took a deep breath, lifted his head high, and strode into Coach Riley's office. The robust, balding coach looked up from behind his metal desk and smiled.

"Ken! It's good to see you, son." The coach motioned to a seat across from him, and Ken sat down. The cramped quarters and dark, fake-wood paneling made Coach Riley look even bigger than he was. Ken waited as the coach scribbled a few notes in a folder, then shoved it aside. "What's on your mind?" he asked.

Ken cleared his throat. "Well, Coach . . . I know you like the direct approach."

Riley nodded once.

"So here it is," Ken said. "I want another chance."

The coach leaned back in his chair, tapping his fingertips together. "I thought we talked about this," he said, his brow furrowed.

Ken edged forward in his seat. "I know. And I remember what you said. But I gotta give it a shot, Coach. I'm ready to play. I'm dying to. I'm not asking for the starting spot or anything. I just want to be back on the team." He heard his foot tapping on the linoleum floor and pressed his forearm into his leg to stop it.

"Ken, listen to me," Coach Riley said calmly. "A lot of people had tough times this fall, but they stuck with it. All I ask of my players is loyalty and effort." He shook his head. "But you quit, Ken. You let the team down."

"I know." Ken swallowed, fighting back a wave of panic. All his arguments flew out the window. "But I'll . . . I'll work twice as hard to make it up to everyone. I'll do whatever it takes."

The coach took a deep breath and slowly let it out. "I can't do it, Ken. Football is not a drop-in sport. How do you think the other players would feel if you joined the team now, after they've been practicing their hearts out this fall?" He calmly opened the folder on his desk. "I'm sorry, Ken, but that's final. I would have loved to have you a month ago, but you made your choice, and you'll have to live with it. Now, unless there's something else I can do for you, I have work to do." He picked up a piece of paper and started reading it.

Ken sagged in his seat. The only sound in the room was the clock on the wall, monotonously ticking away the seconds. *The new sound track to the rest of my life,* he thought. His days as a star athlete were over. He got up and walked out of the room in a daze.

TIA RAMIREZ

I ALWAYS KNEW I WAS LUCKY.
I MEAN, ANY IDIOT CAN SEE
ANGEL IS THE BEST BOYFRIEND
IN THE WORLD. BUT UNTIL TODAY
I NEVER REALIZED HOW LUCKY I
REALLY AM.

SEEING THE COMPLETE HELL
MY FRIENDS ARE PUTTING EACH
OTHER THROUGH MAKES ME
APPRECIATE ANGEL EVEN MORE.
I MEAN, THINK ABOUT IT: DOES
EVEN ONE OF MY FRIENDS
HAVE THEIR PERSONAL LIFE
REMOTELY TOGETHER?

MARIA? ELIZABETH? BOTH
GOT TOTALLY BLINDSIDED BY
CONNER AND ARE STILL
RECOVERING. CONNER? HE'D
RATHER CHEW OFF HIS OWN
FOOT THAN ADMIT THAT HE
CARES ABOUT ELIZABETH.

JESSICA? SHE'S DATING A NICE GUY NOW, BUT I DON'T EVEN KNOW HOW SHE SURVIVED ALL THE ABUSE SHE TOOK FROM MELISSA AND WILL. THE ONLY PERSON I KNOW WHO DOESN'T SPEND EVERY DAY IN EMOTIONAL TORMENT IS ANDY, AND THAT'S PROBABLY BECAUSE THE BOY HASN'T HAD A REAL DATE SINCE EIGHTH GRADE.

SO, HOW DID I END UP SO LUCKY? HOW COME I'M GOING OUT WITH THE CUTEST, SMARTEST, MOST CONSIDERATE PERSON I'VE EVER MET IN MY WHOLE LIFE? I DON'T HAVE A CLUE. BUT I HOPE MY LUCK DOESN'T CHANGE ANYTIME SOON.

CHAPTER 10
Feeling the Rush

Maria sat alone at a table at House of Java, watching the door like a hawk. As soon as Ken walked in, she nearly jumped out of her seat. But one look at his face kept her firmly planted in place. "Ken! What's wrong? What did he say?" she asked as he trudged over and plopped down across from her.

Ken just sat there and sighed. It was like she was looking at an empty husk. The gleam that had been returning to his eyes lately was completely gone.

"Didn't go too well, huh?" Maria asked, starting to feel hollow herself.

"You could say that," Ken muttered.

Maria took a deep breath and closed her eyes. This was all her fault. *What have you got to lose?* she'd asked him. She snuck a glance at his slumped form, his eyes riveted on the mosaic pattern that decorated the top of their table. What did he have to lose? Just his last shred of hope and confidence, apparently.

"What are you having?" she asked. "My treat."

"It doesn't matter." Ken slumped deeper into his chair.

I'd say a double espresso at least, Maria thought. She grabbed one of the waitresses as she walked by and placed the order. They sat in silence until their coffees arrived. Ken didn't move as his steaming cup was placed in front of him, and Maria couldn't take it anymore.

"Okay, so he said no," Maria began, pulling her chair closer to the table. "But at least you gave it your best shot. And you're no worse off than you were before, right?"

"I guess not." He stared at his coffee. Then he finally moved forward in his seat and rested his elbows on the table. "I just . . . I didn't realize before how much I missed football. Now I know I screwed up big time, and there's nothing I can do about it."

Maria took a quick sip of her coffee and set it down. "Maybe there is," she said. "Maybe you should just keep trying until he changes his mind. Never underestimate the power of a good nag." She gave him her most infectious, upbeat smile, but it fell flat.

"You weren't there, Maria." He closed his eyes, obviously reliving the scene. "My football career is over. He was pretty clear about that."

Maria smacked her hand on the table, rattling the coffee cups. Ken looked up, startled. "If you really want to be on the team, I say go . . . be on the team," she said. "I think you should just show up at practice tomorrow, dressed and ready."

Ken stared at her wide-eyed, as if she'd sprouted a new head. "Um, Maria? Have you ever seen my coach? I'd be dead meat."

"What's he gonna do? Tackle you?" She smiled. "You're a football player. I thought you liked that stuff. Besides, maybe all you need is a good pounding to make you feel better."

Ken eyed her skeptically, but a small smile was creeping across his face. "You're insane, you know that?" He shook his head, fiddling with the spoon in his espresso.

"Yeah, well, I bet the coach is dying to have you back," Maria said. "You were first-string all-state last year. He'd be crazy not to give you a shot."

"What about Will?" Ken said.

Maria grinned. "Even a great quarterback like you needs a good backup."

"And the winner is . . . Cobalt, with Shadow Dancer second and Delilah third. Lucky Strike finishes out of the action in fourth. It's Cobalt by a nose, paying three to one."

Angel nodded to himself approvingly. The twelve-to-one long shot he'd bet on, Lucky Strike, had finished out of the money, but Angel still came out ahead because he'd also put twenty dollars on the favorite, Cobalt. It was like insurance. Angel congratulated himself on his savvy strategy and strolled toward the ticket window to collect his winnings.

As he picked his way through the litter-strewn stadium, he felt a little sorry for the people he passed who were glumly tearing up their losing stubs. He had to admit, there were a lot of down-and-outers here. But there were also more than a handful of well-dressed, well-groomed types who looked like they knew exactly what they were doing. He passed one particularly suave-looking guy in a blue blazer who looked just like James Bond. The man was coolly filling out his race card while keeping an eye out to make sure nobody saw his picks. Angel gave him a friendly nod and kept walking. What could he say? Some people had it, and some didn't.

Conner had a point—a lot of people did lose money here. But in every race somebody also had to win. Angel figured his chances had to be at least above average. After all, how many of the people he was betting against were matriculated at Stanford University? He wouldn't be surprised if there was a small group of people like him who were making a steady killing. If he kept at it, maybe he could work his way through college by betting on the horses. He obviously had a knack for it.

He got in line, winning ticket in hand, and felt a warm glow of pride. But as he watched the cashier count out a large stack of bills and hand it to the person in front of him, he couldn't help wishing he had bet more money on Cobalt. By betting only twenty dollars, he had wasted the chance for a real payday. When his turn came, the clerk handed him three twenties without even looking up. Angel walked away quickly, feeling embarrassed. He wouldn't make that mistake again.

Unfortunately he had brought only about eighty dollars with him. That was all that was left of his winnings after his fancy dinner with Tia. Still, he reasoned, he was actually more than six hundred dollars up in his total winnings. If he kept betting only a twenty here and a twenty there, it would take all night to add up to anything.

There was an ATM machine in the stadium, he remembered. He could just . . . no, that was crazy. But if he won it all back, wouldn't the reward be worth the risk? He could find a sure thing and make some real money. He quickly made his way to the ATM and withdrew four hundred dollars from his checking account. After he won a few bets, he would put four hundred aside, and from then on he'd be gambling with the track's money again.

It would feel more comfortable not to be betting from his savings, of course. The best thing would be to win it back quickly but without taking any undue risks. He studied the racing form. The next race had a two-to-one favorite named Old Reliable, with no other horse paying more than seven to one. Angel normally didn't like betting so conservatively because it paid so poorly, but he decided to skip the long shot he had his eye on and put all his money on the favorite. If he bet the whole four hundred dollars, he'd double his money right away, and then he could go back to betting more daringly with his winnings. That seemed like the safest thing to do.

Angel went back to the window and bet four hundred dollars on Old Reliable. Once he came in, the real fun would begin.

Ken pulled on his helmet and snapped the chin strap. He slapped himself on the top of his head hard, tucked in his jersey, and looked at himself in the mirror. Although he was standing in his own bedroom, he could already feel the adrenaline coursing through his veins. It was all coming back—the rush, the feeling of power, how he used to feel almost invincible before a game. He hadn't realized how much he had missed that feeling. When he put on football pads and suited up, he felt like he could take on anyone or anything.

That was what it was going to take too if he really went through with this cockeyed plan. His heart sank as he imagined having to face the coach again. But he had said he didn't like a quitter. Well, maybe Maria was right. Maybe if the coach saw that he refused to give up, he'd realize Ken wasn't a quitter and take him back.

Ken tightened his cleats, pulled off his helmet again, and ran downstairs, wondering if this whole thing was completely crazy. He hadn't even told Maria. He knew that she had only been trying to cheer him up yesterday at House of Java. She would probably think he was nuts if he told her he was actually thinking about going through with her plan. Besides, he hadn't completely made up his mind. It was one thing to put on his gear and look at himself in the mirror. But once he got to the practice field, he wasn't sure he could really get out there.

This was going to be a huge showdown. Ken only hoped that he was really up for it.

Will jogged out of the locker room, psyched to get to practice and get it over with. He knew it was going to be tough to concentrate on the plays when all he could think about was seeing Jessica in a few hours.

"Hey, Simmons!" Will heard Todd Wilkins call from behind him. He kept jogging, knowing Todd would run to catch up. "You gonna try throwing some real passes today?" Todd said when he was shoulder to shoulder with Will.

"Yeah," Will said with a chuckle. "You gonna try catching the ball?"

He was waiting for Todd to come back with another dig, but Wilkins suddenly stopped in his tracks, staring across the freshly watered playing field. Will slowed to a walk and followed Todd's seemingly stunned gaze.

Striding toward them from the far end of the field was a tall player, suited up in a red-and-white SVH uniform.

"There's no number twelve on the team," Will said, checking out the guy's jersey.

"No way," Todd said. Something about his tone made Will's stomach drop.

"Matthews?" someone called out from a group of players who were hanging out by the sidelines.

"I don't believe it," Todd said. He jogged over and slapped hands with Ken, patting him on the back with his free arm. Will stood, watching from a safe distance as SVH players broke away from various groups and joined the crowd forming around Ken. He felt his jaw and fists clench involuntarily. What the hell did Matthews think he was doing?

Glancing around, Will noticed that the El Carro players were all looking on with their hands on their hips. The mutterings had already begun. This didn't look good.

As Will watched his offensive line treating Ken as if he were some kind of rock star, he felt an intense possessiveness creep over him. He'd achieved a good rapport with the SVH linemen—*his* linemen—but it was obviously nothing compared to the affection they still held for their old quarter-back. They were grinning like little kids meeting Santa Claus.

Will strode over to the crowd, feeling the eyes of all his teammates from El Carro following him.

Suddenly Ken spotted him. "Will," he said, his features adopting a placid expression.

"Ken," Will answered, lifting his chin in greeting.

There was a long pause as they stood across from each other.

"Coach didn't mention you'd be trying out," Will said finally. He had tried to sound casual, but there was an edge to his voice he couldn't hide.

Brian Cogley, Will's center, laughed and slapped Ken on the shoulder. "Trying out! The dude was all-state last year, man! As a junior! He doesn't have to try out for his own team."

Will's whole face went red, and he was glad he had his helmet on so no one could see how Brian's turncoat comments affected him. He refused to let his gaze waver from Ken's eyes. Ken blinked first, and Will tried to squelch a smile.

"Look, man, I'm not after your position," Ken said. "I just want to be back on the team."

Several of the El Carro players had come up behind Will, and there were now two distinct groups primed for a face-off. Suddenly a whistle cut through the air. No one spoke or moved so much as an inch as the coach strode up and stood between Ken and Will.

"What the hell is going on here?" Coach Riley demanded.

Ken took a deep breath and looked at Riley. "Coach—"

"What do you think you're doing on my football field, Matthews?" Coach asked in angry amazement.

Ken stepped forward. "You said you didn't like a quitter, Coach. Well, I'm not quitting without a fight. If you want to keep me off the team, you're going to have to drag me off."

"Is that so?" Like a shot, the coach was right in Ken's face. Will had never seen him so mad. His fists were clenched, and veins were bulging on his neck. "Look around you, Ken," Coach demanded through locked teeth. "An hour ago I had a team here. A real team, pulling together for one common goal. It didn't matter whether the guy next to them played for Sweet Valley or El Carro last year. You've been here two minutes, and now look at them." He took a step back and lifted his arms, gesturing at the two opposing groups. "Are you proud of yourself? Is this what you want?"

Ken didn't answer.

The coach looked Ken right in the eye. "There's one thing I hate more than a quitter, Ken. Do you know what it is?"

Ken just stared back. Will was holding his breath

as an ominous silence gripped the field.

"It's a player who puts *himself* above the team," Coach said finally. "I'm disappointed in you, Ken."

Will glanced at Josh Radinsky and Matt Wells, his two best friends. They both looked as stunned and sickened as he felt. None of them wanted Ken on the team, but when someone got a chewing out like that, it hit all the players.

Coach Riley pushed past Ken and addressed the group. "All right, this little distraction has gone on long enough," he barked. "Everyone line up." No one moved. *"Now!"* he yelled. He started striding toward the tackling dummies without a backward glance as the team slowly lined up for calisthenics. No one said a word.

Will let out a sigh and jogged back to his position. A smile started to pull at the corners of his mouth as his friends patted him on the back in support. He wasn't just happy for himself, of course. The team was definitely better off this way.

He glanced back over his shoulder and saw Ken standing in the center of the field, alone.

"Man. Friday nights are the worst," Corey said, tossing her apron on the coffee table. As usual she was wearing black, thrift-shop clothing and a nose ring to match, making her the picture of discontentment.

Jeremy nodded, rubbing his hands over his eyes.

155

They had just spent two hours serving cappuccino to a seemingly endless stream of customers, and he was beat. Corey plopped onto the tattered sofa. "Don't those people have anything better to do on a Friday? I mean, I *have* to be here. What's their excuse?"

"They're nuts," Jeremy said. "For the price of two double lattes they could be eating dinner somewhere." Jeremy sank into one of the frayed new-old armchairs in the House of Java staff room. He could feel a loose spring poking up out of the upholstery and shifted position, unable to get comfortable.

"You've really got to hand it to Ally," he said. "She sure doesn't waste any money on decorating."

"She's taken garage-sale scrounging to whole new levels," Corey said, pulling a tuft of fibers from one of the larger holes in the sofa's armrest.

"Did she get the magazines the same way? I think these are all more than a year old." Jeremy picked up a catalog that lay open on the table. "Wait a minute—this one's new," he said. "Whoa. A furniture catalog? You don't think she's actually considering buying something *new*, do you?"

"No way. It's gotta be for her new apartment," Corey said, swinging up her feet and sprawling out on the full length of the couch.

"You're right. This stuff is way too nice for HOJ," Jeremy said. The catalog was filled with simple, wooden furniture and colorful rugs and tapestries. "You know, Jessica's redecorating," Jeremy said, his eyes falling on a lavender-and-light-green rug that was decorated with huge, abstract flowers. "I should show her this."

"Aw, you're such the good little whipping boy," Corey said sarcastically.

"She's going shopping tomorrow for stuff for her new house," Jeremy said, ignoring her. He reached over, grabbed the beat-up Princess phone from the table, and dialed the number with one hand. Elizabeth answered on the third ring.

"Hi, Liz. It's Jeremy. Is Jessica back yet?"

"No. She left only about a half hour ago, actually," Elizabeth answered. "She has a meeting at First and Ten."

Jeremy's brow furrowed. "Oh. They're at First and Ten?"

"Yeah, that's what she said. She's probably there now if you want to swing by."

"Maybe I'll surprise her after I get out of here," Jeremy said, glancing at his watch.

Elizabeth sighed. "Good idea. She'd probably love to show you off."

Jeremy laughed as they said their good-byes. He rolled the catalog up in one hand and tapped it against his knee. Things were still tense between him and Jessica the last time he saw her. Maybe doing something romantic like surprising her was exactly what they needed to get themselves back on track.

He pushed himself out of his chair and started grabbing boxes from the shelves. He wasn't getting out of here until he stocked the front counter for the late shift. The sooner he got his work done, the sooner he would see Jessica.

Elizabeth Wakefield

Wait a minute. Now that I think about it, in all the years Jessica has been on the team, I don't think she's ever had a cheerleading meeting on Friday night before. And Jessica did seem to be spending a lot of time on her makeup. She did say something about the football team being there, which could explain it—

Oh, no. Not Will.

No. No. It's only a cheerleading meeting. Otherwise why would Tia have just called to say she couldn't make it? And Jessica wouldn't do anything to risk her relationship with Jeremy. . . .

Why am I not remotely comforted?

Why do I care?

One Last Chance

Jessica checked her reflection quickly in the window, then opened the door of First and Ten and plunged into the raucous Friday-night crowd. The din of several competing televisions, all tuned to different sporting events, assaulted her ears. She scanned the room and spotted Will sitting alone at a remote corner table underneath a display of autographed team pennants. Immediately her pulse went into racing mode. *Chill,* she told herself. Maybe if she acted like she wasn't feeling anything, she'd stop feeling everything.

Where was Tia? Jessica had thought she was late enough to guarantee that Tia would get here before her. Jessica took a deep, calming breath, walked quickly through the crowded room, and slid into the chair opposite Will.

"Hey," Will said, smiling.

"Hi," Jessica answered, inadvertently grinning back.

"Did you get the message from Tia?" Will asked.

Jessica froze. "No. What message?"

"She called to say she couldn't make it." Will didn't look at all displeased. "She had to baby-sit at the last minute."

Jessica gripped at her jeans under the table, trying to keep herself from panicking. But she couldn't help it. She had to get out of there, fast.

"I guess we better postpone, then," she said, grappling with her purse, which she'd tossed on the floor under her chair. "She is the captain. . . ."

"Actually, Tia said to go ahead without her and fill her in later. She said she trusts you." Will smiled.

Jessica tried not to groan. This couldn't be happening. It was bad enough meeting Will without telling Jeremy. But if someone saw them *alone* together . . .

At that moment Maria Slater walked up to the table in her black-and-white waitress uniform. When she saw who Jessica was sitting with, she did a double take. "Are you ready to order? Or are you expecting somebody else?" she asked.

"Tia was supposed to be here, but she couldn't make it," Jessica blurted out.

"So it's just the two of us," Will said with a smirk.

Maria looked back and forth between them. "Um . . . okay. What are you having?"

"Nothing. We're really not staying long," Jessica said quickly. "In fact—"

"Well, I'm starving," Will interrupted. "I'll have

162

a burger and fries. Are you sure you don't want anything?"

Jessica's stomach growled, and she sighed. She'd endured a grueling practice that afternoon, and she was famished. "I guess I'll have a burger too," she said. Maria wrote down their order and left, but not before giving Jessica a look and shaking her head ever so slightly. Jessica sank lower into her seat.

"You look . . . really nice, Jess," Will said. Her skin tingled just from the sound of him saying her name, and she almost groaned in frustration. Then he ran his fingers through his hair and stared at the candle.

Jessica shifted in her seat. "We should probably get busy," she said. "I really can't stay too long."

"Right," Will said awkwardly. "Let's get down to business." He leaned forward, placing his elbows on the table, and Jessica almost shrank back. "So, what is this kidnap thing again?" he asked. "Some kind of fund-raiser?"

Jessica smiled in spite of herself. "No. No ransoms are involved." She clasped her hands under the table. That little curl near his collar always made her want to run her fingers through his hair herself. "Basically we just barge into people's rooms early one morning and yank them out of their beds. They all have to go out to breakfast exactly as they are, in their pajamas or . . . whatever."

Will raised his eyebrows. "That could be awkward, couldn't it? I mean, what if you sleep in the raw?"

Jessica felt herself flush. "You get to make yourself decent, but that's all. No brushes, no combs, and definitely no makeup."

"Cheerleaders without makeup. What a concept," he said. "There were some cheerleaders at El Carro who wore so much makeup, you kind of wondered if there was anything else under there."

His smile was infectious, and Jessica couldn't help giggling. "Well, you've never seen my hair in the morning. I look like Medusa."

"That's hard to believe," Will said with a seriousness that made her blush. She picked up a water glass and took a sip in a vain attempt to hide her face. "I'm just glad I'm in on this," he continued. "The last thing I need is for the guys to catch me in my Snoopy boxers."

Jessica almost spit her water out across the table. She started to laugh and covered her mouth with her hand. A little bit of water streamed down her wrist.

"Now *that's* attractive," Will joked, handing her his napkin.

Jessica wiped her face and hands. "You sleep in Snoopy boxers?" she asked with a laugh. Then she noticed Maria standing next to them with their food and quickly pulled herself together.

Maria stared her down. "Can you do me a favor?" she asked. "I'm having trouble with the clasp on my necklace. Could you come to the bathroom with me for a sec?"

"Sure," Jessica said. She shot Will a look that was halfway between apologetic and embarrassed and followed Maria to the bathroom. As soon as the door swung shut, Maria's calm expression vanished. "Have you officially lost your mind?" she asked, crossing her arms over her chest. "What are you doing here with Will?"

"It's not my fault," Jessica said. "We're planning the kidnap. Tia was supposed to be here too, but she bailed."

Maria leaned back against a sink. "You're planning the kidnap," she said skeptically.

"Yeah," Jessica said.

"You were *talking* about his *sleepwear!*" Maria exclaimed.

"I know!" Jessica said, bringing her hands to her forehead. "But it's completely innocent."

"Uh-huh," Maria said, looking Jessica up and down. "That's why you rolled up in here with that little black cardigan on and those come-and-get-me jeans."

Jessica looked down at herself and wrapped her arms over her chest, clutching her right shoulder with her left hand.

"Jeremy is a really nice guy," Maria said, opening the bathroom door. "I just hope you know what you're doing."

So do I, Jessica thought.

*   *   *

Angel felt a lurch in his stomach and leaned forward, afraid he was going to be sick. He stared at the ticket in his hand, then let go of the worthless piece of paper and watched it flutter away in the breeze. Old Reliable had been passed by two horses in the homestretch. Angel sat holding his head in his hands. It was time to rethink the situation.

Obviously he couldn't quit now, with his checking account significantly diminished. But he would definitely lower his sights a little. As soon as he won enough money to replace his savings, he would call it a day and go home.

What he needed was a new strategy. He couldn't afford to place any more big bets on favorites that didn't come in, and small bets on favorites wouldn't pay enough to matter. He'd have to start betting on horses with higher odds.

Excluding a few real long shots, there were four horses in the next race that paid more than four to one. Angel hurried back to the window and bet a little bit of money on all four. One of them had to come in, and then he'd break even. He hurried back to the stands to watch the race, keeping his fingers crossed in his jacket pocket.

This time, however, the favorite won easily. None of his horses finished within five lengths of the leader.

Angel started to sweat. The sun was beating down on him, and he felt like he was being interrogated by

166

a cop shining a bright light in his eyes. It was getting hard to breathe.

Around him he saw people laughing and chatting with their friends, enjoying the afternoon. No one seemed to care that he had just done something incredibly stupid. The loudspeaker was announcing the next race as if nothing had happened.

Angel felt like fleeing out of the stadium and returning to the familiar safety of his room. But he couldn't go home like this. His father was going to kill him.

The thought snapped him awake like a bucket of ice water dumped on his head. If his father found out that Angel had blown half his money at the racetrack, he would never live it down. Angel could win the Nobel Prize, and it wouldn't make any difference. His father would spend the rest of his life telling everyone about the day Angel threw away his hard-earned savings on the horses.

But it didn't have to be like that. He could still win it back. He had enough left to get him over this rough spot. All it would take would be a few good payouts, and no one would have to know it ever happened. Considering the alternative, he didn't really have a choice. Besides, he couldn't keep losing forever. For all he knew, the next race would put him on his feet again, and he would be laughing at himself for having gotten so worried.

The trouble was, he'd reached the limit of

what the ATM would give him from each account in one day. But there was one more card in his wallet.

Reluctantly he pulled out the credit card his father had gotten him for emergencies. It wasn't really like borrowing money to gamble with, he reasoned. He had the money in the bank; he just couldn't get at it. He stuck the credit card in the ATM and withdrew a cash advance.

For the next few races Angel sprinkled bets on several different horses, but they all lost. Every last one. He moved like a zombie, afraid to stop, afraid to think about what was happening as the money flowed through his fingers like sand.

Before he knew it, the loudspeaker was announcing the last race of the day. All Angel had left were a few measly bills.

He scanned the racing form in desperation. Suddenly his heart leaped. There. It was like an omen. Last Chance, paying ten to one. If Last Chance won, Angel would be home free. He had one last chance to win back his savings and pretend nothing had ever happened.

He put all his money on Last Chance and found a seat in the bleachers away from the laughing crowd.

Please, just this one race, he pleaded silently. *If you let me win this one race, I swear I'll never come back to the track again.*

The gun sounded, and the horses dashed out of the gate.

Will sucked the last noisy slurps from the bottom of his milk shake and smacked his lips. "Not bad," he pronounced. "In fact, I think I'll have another."

"Why not?" Jessica said. "I think we've eaten one of everything on the menu. It looks like we don't have much choice but to start repeating things." The table between them was littered with empty glasses and ketchup-stained plates, and the candle in its little football-shaped jar was down to the end of the wick.

Over the last hour Jessica had gradually started to loosen up. As the conversation shifted from the kidnap to other topics, they had started laughing and horsing around, and she had eventually realized she really wasn't doing anything wrong. They were friends.

"It looks like there's just one french fry left," Will said. "You know what that means, don't you?"

"What?" Jessica asked.

"Face-off!"

Jessica raised an eyebrow. "Excuse me? Has the sports theme here gotten to you?"

"It's the only fair way. Put your hands on the table. No, palms down." Jessica did as directed. "Okay, now, on the count of three. One . . . two . . . three!"

Both of their hands shot toward the french fry. Will got there first, but Jessica grabbed his hand and started wrestling him for the fry, which was quickly reduced to a greasy mess. One end was sticking out of his fist, though, and with her free hand, Jessica grabbed it, ripped off a piece, and stuck it in her mouth. "I win!" she yelled.

Suddenly Will's laughter stopped and his face froze, and Jessica looked up. Jeremy was standing right beside them.

His eyes fell on their hands together on the table, and he looked like he'd been punched in the stomach.

"Jeremy!" Jessica said, snatching away her hand. "We were just finishing our meeting—"

"Don't make this any worse than it is," he said.

"Jeremy, please listen to me. Will and I had to organize the senior kidnap—that's all this is. Tia was supposed to be here too, but she couldn't make it. You can ask her tomorrow."

"Don't bother making your friends lie for you too, Jess." He just stared at her for a moment. There was so much hurt in his deep brown eyes, it made Jessica's full stomach turn. Finally he turned and started to walk away.

"Wait!" Jessica cried, standing up and grabbing his wrist.

Jeremy spun around. His expression had shifted to anger, and he yanked his arm away. "I asked you point-blank, and you lied to me. I could tell something was going on, but I still trusted you, even after Melissa told me—"

"Melissa?" Jessica asked, feeling all her senses go on alert. "You heard about this from *Melissa?* How could you even listen to that lying—"

"Who's the liar, Jessica?" Jeremy snapped. "Melissa told me you had a date with Will tonight, and here you are. Did she make all this up too?" He gestured at their empty plates.

Jessica stared at the table. She couldn't deny how it looked. And she couldn't deny to herself that the evening had started to feel like a date. But just the thought of Melissa Fox talking to Jeremy—of her lying to him—of him *believing* her after everything she had put Jessica through . . . all it did was make her angry. Jeremy probably expected her to beg and grovel, but she wasn't going to do it. Not this way.

"*I'm* telling you that this is not a date," Jessica said firmly, looking Jeremy in the eye. Her heart fluttered painfully, but she kept on. "But if you don't even want to give me a second to explain, then don't. If you don't trust me, you might as well leave right now. But if you go, don't bother calling me again."

Jeremy stood rooted to the spot, jaw clenched. He looked from Jessica to Will and back again, then turned and walked away without a word.

Jessica felt hot tears spring to her eyes, and she buried her face in her hands. Maria walked over and hugged her, but it was no use.

Finally Jessica shrugged away from her friend and looked at Will. He was sitting at the table, obviously stunned.

Jessica narrowed her tear-filled eyes at him. "Congratulations, Will," she said bitingly. "Are you happy now?"

". . . And coming into the homestretch, it's Timeless Treasure in first with Legacy back by a length. Chasing them in third is Amazingly Irish, and rounding out the front four is Last Chance. . . ."

Angel stood by the railing, clutching it with all his might as the horses rounded the turn into the homestretch.

"Come on, Last Chance!" Angel screamed at the top of his lungs. "Come on!"

As the horses flashed by, Last Chance seemed to read Angel's desperation. He sped by the pack on the outside and closed in on the leader.

"Timeless Treasure still has the edge, but it's Last Chance coming up fast! Coming up fast!" the announcer called.

"Please, please, *please*," Angel begged.

"And Timeless Treasure is starting to give way. He's opening up the field for Last Chance. . . ."

As the horses thundered down the straightaway,

172

Angel was screaming as loud as he could, and the fans were going wild. Just as Timeless Treasure appeared to be opening up a lead again, he stumbled, and Last Chance surged past him, racing toward the finish line.

"And now it's Last Chance! Last Chance is in first place by a nose. . . ."

Angel breathed a sigh of relief. A few more seconds and the nightmare would be over. He had learned his lesson. He couldn't have come any closer to complete and utter disaster, but he was going to come out of this alive.

"Wait a minute, folks! Streaking in from the back of the field is Black Eagle! Oh, this is unbelievable! Black Eagle and Last Chance are neck and neck!"

Angel's heart hit the bleachers as he watched the dark horse fly by in a blur and pull even with Last Chance. They were running neck and neck, and the crowd was cheering like mad.

Angel held his breath and said a prayer, but it was too late.

"And it's Black Eagle by a nose!" the announcer shouted. "What an amazing race to close out the day, ladies and gentlemen!"

All around Angel people yelled and cheered and waved their winning tickets in the air, but it seemed to Angel as if the commotion were happening somewhere far away. He felt as if he were enclosed in an invisible plastic ball with barely enough air to breathe. Out there, people were putting on their jackets and filing out of the stadium on their way home. Angel sank onto a bench. He felt numb, frozen in a state beyond panic. People streamed past him, but the thought of going home filled him with dread. He could never go back to his comfortable, ordinary life again. It was gone, along with his savings and the respect of his parents. Yesterday he had been a responsible, together guy with a bright future ahead of him at Stanford University. Now he couldn't even afford the gas to get there.

As the crowd thinned out, Angel saw that the stands were sprinkled with people like himself who were sunk in despair, their lives in ruins. One man stumbled by him, blinking back tears and still clutching some losing tickets in his hand. Angel wondered if he had a family. How many people did this happen to each day?

He spotted the snappy dresser he had seen earlier who had reminded him of James Bond. As Angel watched, an usher approached the man and placed his hand on his shoulder. "Come on, Pete," the usher said. "Time to go home." The man got up, gave him a confident nod, and sauntered toward the exit. As he walked nearer, Angel could hear that he was talking to himself. When he walked by, Angel realized the man was talking gibberish.

Something snapped inside him, and Angel sank into a trance. He had no idea how long he sat there that way; the next thing he knew, someone was calling his name.

He turned around and saw Tia and Conner running toward him.

"What are you doing here?" he said, confused.

"You were supposed to meet us two hours ago!" Tia said. "Why didn't you call? I was worried about you!"

Angel was speechless.

"Yeah, man, I thought you were only coming for a couple of hours," Conner said.

Tia sat down on the bench next to him and looked in his eyes. "What's wrong, sweetie?" she said.

A single tear rolled down Angel's cheek.

"My God, Angel. What happened?"

Conner pulled the ticket from his hand. "A hundred sixty dollars?" he said skeptically. "I thought you were here to catch some sun."

"Angel, did you just waste a hundred and sixty dollars on a stupid bet?" Tia demanded. "That's a lot of money! How could you—"

Angel buried his head in his hands and started to sob. Tia wrapped her arms around him. "It's okay," she said. "It's not that bad." Angel just moaned.

"Angel? Exactly how much money did you lose

tonight?" Conner asked, his voice sounding dead. Tia pulled away and looked at his face.

"All of it." It came out barely more than a whisper.

"What do you mean, 'all of it'?" Tia asked slowly.

"It's all gone. All the money I saved this summer," he said. "All of it. Gone."

KEN MATTHEWS

8:56 P.M.

My football career is now officially over. It looks like my future depends completely on my academics.

I might as well start learning to pump gas.

JEREMY AAMES
9:22 P.M.

My life has officially hit bottom. Unless my car catches on fire, things could not get any worse.

On the bright side, at least now I know I wasn't imagining things. So I'm not going insane.

That's a big plus.

JESSICA WAKEFIELD

10:03 P.M.

This time I know I have no one to blame but myself.

The weird thing is, now the one person in the world who doesn't think I'm a lying, cheating slut is Will. Ironic, huh? If that's the best I can do for friends, I guess I've sunk pretty low.

ANGEL DESMOND

10:27 P.M.

Tomorrow morning I am going to lose my father's respect forever. Because that's when I have to tell him what I've done, and my life will never be the same again. If I even have a life, that is. Tia is probably going to kill me first.

TIA RAMIREZ

10:32 P.M.

I WOULD KILL ANGEL, BUT I
DON'T THINK I'LL GET A CHANCE.
HIS FATHER WILL FIRST.

Check out the **all-new**....

(Sweet Valley Web site—)

www.sweetvalley.com

New Features

Cool Prizes

The **ONLY** official Web site!

Hot Links

.... (And much more!)

Bantam
Bantam Doubleday Dell

BFYR 202

You'll always remember your first love.

Love Stories

Looking for signs he's ready to fall in love?

Want the guy's point of view?

Then you should check out *Love Stories*. Romantic stories that tell it like it is—why he doesn't call, how to ask him out, when to say good-bye.

Love Stories

Available wherever books are sold.